Wrong Swipe

A Modern Love Story in the Age of Endless Options

By

Verses Voyage

ISBN : 978-93-344-4930-3

Cover Design: Verses Voyage

Dedication

To the unseen mentor whose art taught me that truth speaks loudest in silence, and that emotion, when sculpted with precision, becomes timeless.

If even a fragment of that mastery has touched these pages, it remains my quiet blessing.

Verses Voyage

Destiny runs on slow Wi-Fi.
We keep refreshing, thinking love will load faster the next time.

Reader Promise

A witty, heart-tugging romantic comedy about pride, partnership, and second chances.

In the rush of Delhi's metros, meetings, and mixed signals, two modern hearts discover that some wrong swipes are really the universe nudging you right.

Every **Verses Voyage** story promises:

- Love that feels lived-in, not idealized.
- Characters who stumble, stay, and grow, just like us.
- Dialogues that echo the conversations you've already had in your head.
- Hope that outlasts silence.
- And words that remind you: sometimes the truest fiction is born from real feelings.

Meet the Cast (and the Chaos)

as introduced by Aarav Mehta

Hi, I'm **Aarav Mehta.**

Startup founder. Certified overthinker. Half logic, half impulse, full chaos. I wake up with ambition, sleep with self-doubt, and survive on sarcasm.

Dreams of changing the world usually end with me changing PowerPoint slides.

My family says I chase ideas like they're auto-rickshaws, loud, fast, and usually taken.

Rhea says I treat emotions like startup pitches, overexplained and underdelivered.

Still, I believe in stories, and in Wi-Fi that reconnects after every crash.

Rhea Sharma

Marketing wizard. Grammar ninja. The kind of person who colour-codes emotions and proofreads the universe.

Her smile could launch campaigns; her silence could end them. She plans everything except me, logic dressed like laughter, strategy hiding a heartbeat.

Some people make eye contact; she makes project plans and somehow, I still blink first.

Pranav Mehta

My elder brother, part-time philosopher, full-time trouble. Runs our family like a start-up: loud, loving, mostly functional.

Aditi Mehta

My sister-in-law and the household's Wi-Fi of reason.

Keeps peace with chai and perfectly timed one-liners.

Simran Sharma

Rhea's younger sister. Runs on caffeine, gossip, and the conviction that she's destiny's intern.

Mr. & Mrs. Mehta

My parents. Old-school romantics who think stability is sexier than spontaneity. Their favourite app? Shaadi.com.

Mr. & Mrs. Sharma

Rhea's parents. Proud, practical, and professional match-fixers of every festival season.

I'm telling this story, the wrong swipes, the right silences, and the bits everyone pretends never happened.

So grab a coffee, a charger, and an open mind. Because everything that follows is proof that even the universe has a sense of humour.

Our Journey Ahead

If a page makes you pause, smile, or forgive yourself a little, that's the promise kept.

Contents

Chapter 1

The Wrong Swipe

Some accidents don't bruise; they bloom.

The Café, somewhere in Delhi

"Arav! Cappuccino!"

The barista shouted my name like breaking news on Aaj Tak, one A missing, confidence included.

Half the café turned; no one cared.

Foam hissed, a toddler screamed, someone's MacBook crashed under the weight of ambition.

Delhi at peak morning bandwidth.

I, Aarav, with two A's, was waiting for a Tinder date that already felt like an HR interview powered by caffeine.

First dates on apps are product demos: you hope the glitch doesn't appear in Version 1.

I checked my reflection in the glass door.

Hair : Rebellious.

Shirt: Confused between "cool founder" and "accountant on Casual Friday."
Confidence : Buffering.

Entrance

Then the door chimed.
She walked in.
White shirt, fitted jeans, hair tied in a bun that meant business. Every step said she didn't need to be here, but I still wanted her to.
Calm face, quiet authority.
Her heels clicked like punctuation, full stop... full stop... question mark.
Rhea...From the app. Only realer.
She scanned the café like a critic reviewing ambience for sincerity. Then her eyes found me.
Time didn't stop; it just cleared its throat and waited.
Sunlight trailed behind her, painting the ends of her hair gold. Even the coffee machine exhaled quietly, as if the city wanted to hear what happened next.
I stood. Too fast.
Banged my knee on the table. Baptised my phone in cappuccino.
She paused, eyebrow raised.
"Smooth."
"Phone was shivering," I said. "*Offering warmth.*"

Her lips twitched, a half-smile, dangerous and involuntary, that stayed just long enough to feel like luck had glanced my way. It was the emotional equivalent of hitting a last-over six by accident, pure relief, pure disbelief, and enough to keep me in the match.

She shook her head, amused despite herself, and sat.

The Conversation Begins

"So this is your idea of hello? Coffee baptisms?"

"Premium service. VIP list only."

"Oh? Lucky me."

"Careful. There's a surcharge for sarcasm."

The waiter appeared. "Arav? Anything else?"

"It's Aarav, two A's."

He nodded gravely, like peace had been restored to the alphabet, and left.

"You really care about that extra A," she said.

"That A has done more branding for me than my start-up."

She laughed. "At this rate, they'll print it on your visiting card, Aarav, with two A's and one full-time branding issue."

Silence arrived, exam-hall silence. Even my coffee looked nervous. She rescued me.

"Sorry I'm late. Parking drama. One uncle refused to reverse, said God was testing his patience."

"I already failed round one," I said, wiping cappuccino off my phone, "spilled before the date even started."

She smiled. "Strong start. Maybe God's still testing you too."

A baby threw another biscuit. Missed again. Hopeful kid.

We spoke together:

"You look, "/ "Is that your real, "

We stopped. Laughed. The kind of laugh that feels like relief disguised as chemistry.

Connection unlocked. Level One.

Outside the window, the city kept rushing, but our table had quietly stepped out of time.

Inside the Conversation

"So... wrong swipe or lucky one?" she asked. "You boys swipe fast, then blame destiny when all you get is regret and cold coffee."

"If this is regret, I'll take the repeat, with you, of course. Some mistakes deserve a sequel."

"Good save."

We talked. Slowly at first, then freely.

She's Delhi-born, a marketing strategist juggling clients who treat "urgent" like religion.

I'm Ahmedabad-bred, chasing a start-up dream that mostly chases me back.

"You use 'founder' like a surname," she teased.

““Says the woman who treats her planner like a GPS for life. You colour-code your life?” I shot back.

Tabs peeked out of her notebook, a rainbow of control.

“Of course. Blue for work, green for family, yellow for friends, pink for emergencies.”

“Emergencies get pink?”

“Red’s too dramatic. Chaos deserves good stationery.”

She said it like a woman who could alphabetise your heart for sport.

“So every emotion has a shade?”

“Doesn’t yours?”

“Mostly coffee-coloured. Occasionally panic grey.”

She looked at my cup. “Add trouble brown.”

Her laugh came quick and bright, the kind that bends heads without asking permission.

For a moment I wondered if she’d rehearsed that poise, or if life just obeyed her planner.

“Better than living in a folder called Miscellaneous,” she said.

“Order’s overrated,” I replied, gesturing at my stained shirt. “Abstract expressionism.”

She blinked, then laughed again, glass-bright, effortless.

The café stilled for half a second, like Delhi itself had leaned in. She didn’t care. Neither did I.

Between Lines

We drifted to family and parents who still think Shaadi.com is a government department.

"Apps everywhere," I said. "They've basically become the ministry of modern life, finance, food, even feelings."

Rhea laughed. "True. And our parents still think Shaadi.com comes with a lifetime warranty and a marriage certificate."

"Yeah," I said. "For them, it's less an app, more a government scheme : log in once, never log out till mission accomplished."

She shook her head, laughing mildly, which committed light crime on the air.

Then she leaned in, chin resting on her palm, her eyes calm but intent, the kind that hold you a second too long.

"Biggest fear?"

There's always one heartbeat between comfort and confession.

"Being average forever," I said.

Her smile softened, the kind that glows, not flashes. "Same."

We stared at the table, pretending the air hadn't just changed texture. The silence stretched, not awkward, just aware. Then she reached for her bag, smile returning like a curtain half drawn.

"Well," she said finally, "that was... something."

"Seven on entertainment," I said.

"Four on privacy."

"Ten on memes."

That broke her guard. A low laugh, unplanned, perfect.

The café noise faded. Screens dimmed. Just the quiet proof of connection.

Outside

I walked her to her car.

Gulmohar petals carpeted the road, Delhi's idea of romance, outsourced to trees.

"Meet again?" I asked, *too casual to be casual.*

"Maybe."

Half-smile. Half-promise.

I held the gate open as she stepped through, the evening air thick with all the things we hadn't said.

When she leaned into the car, the distance between us vanished for a breath, her scent brushed past me, citrus, jasmine, and something dangerously close to hope.

I wanted to bottle it, label it "*Maybe*".

She paused, turned slightly.

"Aaa-rav..." she whispered, letting the first syllable linger like a sigh, the second A stretching just enough to sound like a heartbeat.

I heard it clearly, the two A's, soft yet certain, as if she'd underlined my name with breath.

For a moment, even the city seemed to hold its noise, unsure whether to interrupt or applaud.

Then her car rolled away, leaving petals, exhaust, and *one very confused man,* me, trying to decode the algorithm of destiny.

Love-Guru Broadcast

Phone buzz.

Pranav (Love Guru): How was it?

> (For context: my elder brother, Pranav, married to Aditi, who's equal parts wit and patience. He's smug, confident, and utterly convinced he's a relationship expert just because he's survived three anniversaries without sleeping on the couch. Together, they treat my love life like their favourite weekend project.)

Me: Wrong swipe. Played it cool.

Pranav: Translation, you spilled something?

Me: Half a cappuccino. Full dignity loss.

Pranav: Good sign. Confused girls call back.

Me: You've been married too long to give dating advice.

Pranav: Exactly why I'm qualified.

Then came his voice note, deep, pseudo-sage:

> *"Love-Guru Rule #7: If coffee spills but she still smiles, the universe just gave you a hint. Don't mess it up."*

I laughed into the emptying café. "Trust you to turn caffeine into destiny."

Split Screen

Traffic crawled. Delhi hummed like an exhausted song.

Rhea's phone buzzed on the seat beside her. She let it.

The evening replayed, coffee spilling like nerves, bad jokes sprinting for dignity, that boyish sincerity hiding behind startup jargon.

No violins. No filters. Just awkward pauses and too much caffeine.

And still, somewhere between two red lights, she smiled.

Not because he was perfect, but because for one unplanned hour, she'd been allowed to be herself, unfiltered.

She had laughed without checking her reflection first.

Maybe that was his real trick, he made her forget the need to stay in control.

The signal turned green. She didn't move. The city honked its impatience; she smiled anyway, soft, private, like a secret still loading.

Maybe it wasn't love. Maybe just relief. Either way, it felt good to feel again.

Closing Beat

Some accidents don't bruise. They bloom. Love had barely left the café.

Next Day, by breakfast, Maa logged into Shaadi.com. By dinner, destiny was double-booked.

Maybe love isn't about finding someone new; maybe it's about seeing someone in a better light.

Chapter 2

Shaadi.com Shock

When family networks outsmart neural networks.

The Pitch Meeting No One Approved

Sunday afternoons at our place mean two things: naps for the sane, and matchmaking for my mother.

I was halfway to dreamland, auditing my past dating errors, when Maa's voice cut through the steam.

"Beta, wear a nice shirt. Not that faded one."

That sentence, in any Indian home, signals the arrival of a trap.

"Why?"

"Because we're meeting a nice girl."

Tone: TV-anchor-announcing-budget-speech.

"Shaadi.com sent good profiles. I liked one. Five o'clock. Imperial Spice."

I sat up, alert as breaking news.

"You fixed a marriage interview without telling me? Did you not notice I just deleted Tinder yesterday?"

"Don't be dramatic," she said. "It's just coffee."

"With aunties, uncles, and biodata laminated like passports?"

"Exactly! And your horoscope is trending high, Aarav. Don't waste planetary alignment."

Dad rustled his newspaper, the universal symbol for I am neutral; feed me later.

"Maa, you're not finding me a wife, you're casting me in a Sooraj Barjatya sequel."

"At least those films end happily. Your dating life is still in beta version."

I sighed. "I'm not wearing formals."

"Wear them."

"Sandals."

"Aarav."

"Compromise: sneakers. Smart-casual code."

She muttered, *"Your generation will marry in sneakers only*, I swear."

Imperial Spice, 5 p.m.

Golden chandeliers. Soft ghazals. Waiters gliding like they'd trained with swans.

The place smelled of ghee, hope, and financial scrutiny.

Maa and Dad sat beside me, radiating optimism brighter than the lighting budget.

"Sit straight," Maa whispered. "Smile more. We must show high ROI."

"I'm not a showroom dummy."

"Exactly. Dummies sell faster."

The door opened. A family entered, father in beige blazer, mother in silk saree, and between them... her.

Rhea.

The coffee-spill casualty from Tinder.

The emoji glitch in my operating system.

She froze mid-step. I forgot how to breathe.

Her eyes said, No way. Mine said, Rollback to Version 0.1.

Maa, blissfully unaware:

"Beta, this is Rhea, very nice girl, marketing job, Delhi background."

"We've... met. Yesterday," I croaked.

Her father blinked. "Already? Where?"

"Yes," Rhea said smoothly. "Accidentally. Minor traffic incident."

Menus arrived, decorative, irrelevant. Parents don't need menus; they bring questionnaires.

The Interview

Mrs Sharma opened with a smile sharpened by experience.

"So, you are in IT?"

"Sort of," I said. "I run a start-up. Early phase."

Her husband adjusted his cufflinks, gesture decoded as unstable income detected.

"What exactly does it do?"

"We've built an MVP, pilot clients, scaling soon. Basically, survival with ambition."

His nod translated to : *"Unemployed but Hopeful."*

Rhea hid a laugh behind the menu.

"And income?" he pressed.

"Papa," she hissed.

"What? Practical questions must be asked. We are discussing a long-term contract, not a casual fling."

Maa jumped in like a referee. "He's hardworking! Top college. Good boy. No drinking, no smoking, fixes Wi-Fi."

"Maa," I muttered, "you're describing an IT saint."

Mrs Sharma brightened. "Both Libras , perfect match!"

"Perfect," Rhea echoed, stabbing her papad like it owed her money.

Under the table her pointed shoe nudged my sneaker.

A silent alliance.

Two developers maintaining legacy code.

"So, Rhea," I said, "hobbies? Apart from generating parking drama and confusing apps?"

Her eyes flashed. "Traffic drama," she corrected. "And my apps work perfectly."

The waiter appeared. "Arav? Cookies?"

"It's Aarav , two A's."
Rhea smirked. "Consistency really is your brand."

The Parents Collab

Maa, leaning forward: "See, you two look so comfortable!"
"Maa, we were traumatised together. That's a different bonding model."
Dad choked on his water.
Her father cleared his throat. "Good to see youngsters laugh. Laughter keeps marriage alive."
Rhea's smile turned diplomatic. "So does mutual respect."
Silence. Priceless.
Her mother tried rescue. "At least both are independent. Modern thinking."
The waiter returned with gulab jamuns: the peace offering of all awkward dinners.

The Subtext War

Small talk tip-toed through territory mined with expectations.
Rhea's father: "What's your five-year plan?"
Me: "Growth, stability, scaling."
Him: "Personal?"
Me: "Same. Different department."
Maa beamed. "See? He plans!"
Rhea's voice, calm: "Plans change."

Her mother smiled, half-warning. "Yes beta, but stability is important."

Rhea met my eyes. See? Your turn to speak.

I swallowed my courage with the water. "Sometimes growth needs risk," I said. "Even start-ups need trust investors."

Maa's spoon paused mid-air. "Beta trust is fine, but EMI is real."

Everyone laughed except Rhea and me.

We were busy surviving irony.

Exit Protocol

Dessert ended. So did grace.

Parents exchanged smiles that meant potential but pending due diligence.

Outside, under the Imperial Spice signage, I exhaled. Her family moved toward their car; my parents toward theirs. Rhea lingered near the stairs, clutch loose.

"You could've warned me," she whispered.

"Believe me, I tried. Maa's faster than Wi-Fi."

"Next time, make the warning pop-up stronger."

"*Next time*?" I asked, *hopeful.*

She rolled her eyes. "Don't read between the lines. It's bad for business."

Pause. Then softer:

"Still... thanks for surviving that meeting without crashing the server."

"Likewise," I said. "We're good beta-testers."

Her cab pulled up. Before leaving, she looked back once, not dramatic, just real.

"Fix your code, Aarav," she said. "Some bugs cost more than coffee."

And she was gone.

Split Screen

Aarav - Home, Night

Maa was on call with Mrs Sharma, conducting what sounded suspiciously like a merger review.

"Lovely girl, good family, perfect horoscope sync."

Pranav muttered, "You just turned a date into due diligence."

Aditi whispered, "He'll survive. He's already emotionally IPO'd."

I stared at my phone. No message.

The silence felt like a pending update.

Rhea - Car Ride Home

Her parents debated in soft murmurs.

"Nice boy," her mother said.

"Unstable career," her father countered.

"Good smile."

"Still unstable."

She watched the road blur into orange.

He was clumsy, nervous, oddly sincere, a human error she didn't mind debugging.

Maybe fate was lazy but creative, recycling leads until they clicked →

Sometimes we meet the right person at the wrong time, again and again, until the universe decides to get it right.

Epilogue

At the Mehta house, Maa triumphantly typed, "Meeting successful" into the family group.

At the Sharma home, Rhea stared at her planner, then wrote one line under Monday:

Check app again. Maybe.

And the algorithm chuckled somewhere in the cloud.

Because destiny, like all Indian families, hates unfinished business.

Chapter 3

Table for Four, Trouble for Two

Parental diplomacy meets
premature chemistry.

Operation Rishta Revival

Disasters in my life usually begin with Maa's phone and unlimited enthusiasm.

After the "coffee meeting" with Rhea, I assumed the universe had cracked its joke and moved on.

Maa, however, treats coincidences like franchise opportunities.

By nightfall she and Mrs Sharma had discovered each other on WhatsApp.

By midnight they had exchanged birth charts, blood groups, and three versions of "Jai Shri Krishna."

By morning a "friendly dinner" was confirmed so the families could get "better acquainted."
Friendly dinner = trial exam for marriage, with food instead of mercy.

Imperial Spice, Reloaded

Same restaurant. Same chandeliers.
Different stakes.
I had ironed my kurta into obedience; Dad had prepared "casual" questions like a viva examiner practising empathy.
Rhea entered with her parents, calm face, storm eyes. Her dupatta behaved better than my pulse.
We took our places: two sets of parents, two involuntary volunteers.
"Lovely to meet again," Mrs Sharma sang.
"Lovely," Maa echoed, the parental code for deal closing today.
Papads cracked like stress relievers.
"So, Aarav," her mother began, "hobbies?"
Before I could answer, Maa beamed,
"He reads the Gita every morning!"
I choked. "Maa, "
Rhea sipped water, amused. "Balanced mindset."
Her father nodded. "Balance is good. Career, marriage, everything."
Rhea's fingers tightened around her spoon. "Balance needs two people, Papa."

The waiter arrived in mercy.

Dinner with Lag Time

"Income stable?" her father asked.

"Stable-ish," I said. "Like bitcoin, volatile but promising."

Polite laughter made a short round trip.

Rhea bit her lip to hide a smile.

Maa leaned forward. "Rhea beta, you cook also na? Very important for a happy home."

Table braced.

"Sometimes, Aunty," Rhea said softly. "But cooking isn't a test of a good girl. It's a skill, like Excel. You hire for it if you need."

Dad nodded gravely. "Excel is important. *Very stable.*"

Maa blinked, regrouping. "Yes, yes. Basic functionalities check only."

Rhea's smile was polite; her eyes weren't. The baby at the next table began its encore, chaos disguised compassion.

I reached for the chaas and, as tradition demands, spilled half of it. Rhea dabbed her kurta, half-laughing.

"Some men bring flowers. You bring dairy disasters."

"Limited-edition romance," I said.

Parents misread sarcasm as chemistry, thank God for optimists.

Food arrived, paneer butter masala, dal makhni, naans puffed with hope.

Our parents ate with focus and like peace negotiators; we whispered like smugglers.

I slid a folded napkin toward her: Escape plan? Fake food poisoning?

She scribbled back without looking up: Only if you drink the chilli chutney neat.

I raised a brow. She tried not to laugh. *Failed.*

That laugh, small, genuine, mine for half a second.

“Wedding halls are getting booked fast,” her father announced to no one in particular.

Maa brightened. “Winter is auspicious! Good date for *full release* (marriage ceremony).”

I cleared my throat. “So are start-ups. We’re still in developer build.”

Silence did a slow lap around the table.

Rhea broke it, steady and clear.

“Uncle, Aunty, we’re still getting to know each other. If something serious is here, we’ll say it, not our horoscopes.”

Her mother looked surprised, then quietly proud.

Maa looked at me like: Learn from this girl. She knows stakeholder management.

Exit Interview

Dessert arrived, all decorative guilt.

Parents downgraded from ambition to small talk, schools, traffic, petrol prices.

Under the table, Rhea's foot brushed mine, not flirty, ally-like. A truce signed in silence.

We stood. Parents drifted ahead; we lingered by the door.

"Thank you," I said.

"For what?" "For the Excel line. And for saving me from drowning in chaas."

"You create too many bugs," she said, half smiling.

"I'm adaptable."

"Stable-ish," she replied. "Like bitcoin."

"For once, let's hope I appreciate in value."

Her smile lasted till the door opened.

Delhi evening outside, amber, dusty, almost kind.

"Next time," she said, "no dairy stunts."

"No guarantees," I said. "That's the beauty of beta testing."

She shook her head, laughing despite herself. "Goodnight, Aarav."

She said it with two A's. I counted.

The developer build had survived another test, so had we. Still buggy, still running, but somehow, still online.

Some connections don't advance by proposal; they sneak forward through shared sarcasm and spilled chaas.

Parallel Nights

Aarav, Later That Night Back home, the post-mortem began.

Pranav poured kulfi like truth serum.

"So, you like her."

"I respect her," I said.

Pranav : "Good at client handling. Translation: *you like her*."

Aditi grinned. "Honesty works better than PowerPoint."

Maa called from the kitchen: "Nice girl! Knows Excel!"

Family echoed. I surrendered.

Rhea, Later That Night

"Simran!" Mrs Sharma called from the kitchen.

Her younger daughter appeared in the doorway, hoodie, headphones, half a smile.

If Rhea was order and deadlines, Simran was chaos wrapped in charm: the kind of sister who quoted memes instead of advice and still managed to be right most of the time.

"Dinner's ready," Mrs Sharma said. "And no phone at the table."

"I was researching human behaviour," Simran replied, already scrolling again.

Dinner table debrief.

Father: "Ambitious boy. Needs steady partner."

Mother: "Charming smile."

Simran: "Chaotic cute. Keep."

Rhea pretended to check email, smiling at the screen instead.

Later that night she placed her planner on the desk.

Under Tuesday she wrote:

Project follow-up call with Aarav. Carry sugar packets.

She closed the book, still smiling.

Chapter 4

Bazaar of Mix-Ups

One bazaar, two baskets, unlimited misunderstandings.

Market Economics

Sunday mornings in Delhi mean two things, heat and haggling. I had both in generous supply.

Maa handed me a list that read like a government tender:

Two kilos marigold.

Five malas.

Roses, if fresh.

Bargain properly.

Translation: don't return without proof of extreme effort, or the household operating system fails.

The flower bazaar smelled of marigolds, incense, and mild regret. Vendors shouted prices like cricket commentators, "Dus ka mala! Bees ka do!"

A cow, unimpressed, chewed someone's profit margin.

Delhi at its best, chaotic, fragrant, alive.

Collision Detection

I reached for a bright bundle of marigolds, the exact orange Maa calls "maximum prosperity."

Another hand reached the same moment.

We froze. Same flowers, same confusion.

She looked up. *Rhea.*

Loose cotton kurta, sleeves rolled, hair tied. The universe's favourite rerun.

"Office event," she said before I could ask.

"Puja at home," I replied. "Maa's orders. *Maximum-security protocol.*"

We both held the same bundle of marigolds. Neither let go.

"I saw it first." "My hand touched first." "Possession is nine-tenths of the law."

"Digital timestamp proves otherwise."

The vendor grinned. "Couple discount!"

"Not a couple!" we said together.

The cow snorted, unimpressed.

Finally, she took half, I took half. Hers looked brighter. Obviously.

Mixed Inventory

"Yours are vitamin-enriched," I said.

"Because I chose them," she replied.

"Bias!"

"Skill."

She turned to the next stall. I followed.

A scooter honked; her dupatta snagged on a rusty nail. I freed it carefully. "Service included. Free software patch."

"Thanks," she said, almost smiling.

Her phone rang. "Yes, I have the flowers. Relax, I'm managing dependencies."

I grinned. "You sound like a CEO."

"Somebody has to be. My office runs on perfection, not hopes and wishes."

"Must be exhausting." "Excellence always is."

For a second her face softened, like even perfection needed air. Then she pointed at the vendor and looked at me. "Kitne Malas chahiye (how many garland)?"

"I'll take ten," I said.

"I'll take fifteen," she said.

The vendor counted. "Sirf pandrah bache hain (only 15 left)."

Quick calculation. No win-win possible.

Rhea spoke before I could. "*Ten for me, five for him.*"

"You just overruled me!" "You just over-ordered."

She pointed at the list in my hand. "That's your mother's handwriting. You need five, not ten."

I blinked. "You read that upside down."

"I'm fluent in maternal."

The vendor laughed, tying bundles. "Strong couple. Good understanding."

"Not a couple!"

The vendor handed over fifteen malas and tucked a jasmine gajra into her basket. "Gift for sister."

The cow mooed again, doubting us.

Marigold Mayhem

As we paid, a scooter splashed through a puddle.

We jumped aside, collided, and our baskets toppled.

Garlands rolled across the road like escaped suns.

"Great," she said. "Now prosperity is public property."

We both bent to gather them.

Our fingers brushed. Static. Moment. Chaos.

The vendor shook his head. "Strong thread, stronger heart."

Rhea burst out laughing, helpless, bright, contagious.

I joined in, ridiculous and happy.

For one strange instant, under the noise and the stink of petrol, it felt like something sacred had elbowed its way into Delhi traffic.

Auto Mode

At the auto stand, one rickshaw waited.
"You take it," she said.
"You take it," I said.
The driver started the meter, end of debate.
We climbed in.
Her basket on the seat, mine on the floor, *balance of power was confirmed.*
Rhea adjusted the jasmine so it wouldn't crush.
The driver spat "Gutka" with Olympic precision.
Bazaar noise faded as the auto moved.
"Rule one of bargaining?" I asked.
"Don't blink."
"Two?"
"Smile."
"Three?" "Carry change."
"Four?"
"Never reveal your budget."
"Graduated with honours," I said.
She smiled. "Do that in your start-up culture too. Might save you from investors."
We hit a red light.
A boy selling roses tapped the auto frame. "One for madam?" "Madam buys her own flowers," she said.
I paid anyway. "Consider it user feedback."
She rolled her eyes, but her smile betrayed her.

Drop Point

At the junction she stepped out.

I picked up a jasmine gajra and her basket. Held it out to her.

“For yourself,” I said.

Her brows lifted, half surprise, half warmth.

“Thanks, Aarav.”

Cherished.

She walked away, basket steady, sunlight catching her hair. Delhi blurred around her, the city briefly kind.

Parallel Feeds

Aarav - Later

Maa inspected the flowers like exam copies.

“Good. Fresh. You bargained?”

“With destiny,” I muttered.

Rhea – Office

The jasmine lay on her desk, not for the event, just hers.

Emails pinged; colleagues shouted deadlines.

She tuned them out.

Somewhere in her planner, between venue audit and vendor call, she scribbled:

Check app with Aarav.

Then, smaller: a doodled smiley.

Rhea's Note

Her parents' voices floated from last night, stability, prospects, practicalities.
She let them fade.
What stayed was smaller:
The sound of laughter spilling across puddles and a boy who didn't hide when things went wrong.
Not perfect.
Not planned.
Just real.

Chapter 5

Swipe vs Shaadi Debate

A metro coach becomes a TED Talk on modern love.

The Commute Begins

The Delhi Metro at 9 a.m. is a battlefield disguised as public transport.

People don't commute; they compete. It's the city's daily stress test, no syllabus, no mercy.

I stepped in with one mission: find a seat before the swarm hit. And there it was, a single shining rectangle under the tube light, a throne of temporary peace.

Then she appeared from the other door. Same target. Same glint.

We charged.

A schoolboy darted between us and claimed it. Algorithm favoured youth.
Rhea straightened, strands escaping her bun, half breath, half laughter.
"You're thirty and still losing to minors?"
"I let him win. Building long-term karma."
"Generous. Saint Aarav of the Standing Compartment. Holiness by helplessness. Delhi's latest miracle."
The train lurched; we grabbed the same handrail. One bar, two hands, shared democracy of metal and fingers.
Perfume, sweat, ambition, all mixing like life's default cologne.
Someone's phone blared Kala Chashma.
Someone else sighed about EMI.
Delhi moved, half awake, half dreaming.

The Debate Sparks

"So..." she said, over the rattle, "about that dinner."
"Which one?"
"The one with four parents and zero oxygen. Our Developer Build dinner."
"Ah, yes, the *merger meeting*. Equal shareholders, unequal panic."
Her smile returned, slow and measured. "Tell me honestly, do these apps make love stupid?"

"Sometimes," I said. "They definitely make it faster. And more disposable. But also, possible."

"Possible for what?"

"To meet people, you'd never meet otherwise. To expand your circle beyond your mother's contact list."

"Like us?"

"Exactly."

She nodded, eyes on the window. "Still dodging your mother's matchmaking army?"

"She's relentless. Shaadi.com is her fantasy league."

"My dad thinks Tinder is the beginning of civilisation's collapse."

"For families, maybe. For curiosity, not bad. Low-commitment beta testing."

She raised an eyebrow. "You call spilt coffee and a shared chaas disaster beta testing?"

"Scientific experiment. Result: chemistry observed, commitment pending."

She shook her head. "You're incorrigible."

"Compliment accepted."

The Interruption

At Mandi House, a man selling phone covers sang Kishore Kumar so badly the original would've sued. An uncle lowered his newspaper just enough to glare.

"In our time," he declared, "people didn't discuss love in trains. We got married and learned to adjust. Stability was the only metric."

Rhea smiled, polite but unafraid. "And were you happy, Uncle?"

He blinked, surprised. "We managed. We didn't expect fireworks. Stability was enough."

"That's the difference," she said softly. "You built love after marriage. We're trying to find it before. We want the love before the launch."

Uncle grunted. "Your apps, fast-food emotions. Swipe today, forget tomorrow."

"Maybe," she said. "But at least we choose our own meal. You had fixed menus designed by your parents."

A few passengers chuckled.

Uncle softened, curiosity replacing judgment. "Choice isn't everything. Too much choice confuses the heart. Decision fatigue."

"True," she said, "but no choice suffocates it. You call it peace; sometimes it's paralysis."

He looked up properly now, eyes less stern. "In my day, people didn't leave at the first crack. We repaired. We tolerated."

"Maybe you tolerated more than you repaired," she said.

"You kept the house standing, but how many rooms went dark inside?"

The carriage fell silent, the kind of silence that listens.

Uncle's voice dropped. "And now? You exit at the first crack."

She nodded. "Because we grew up watching those dark rooms. We just want windows this time, air, light. If we stay, we want to choose it, not endure it."

He considered, then smiled faintly. "Maybe both sides are right. You want meaning; we wanted continuity. Love probably needs both."

Rhea smiled back. "Continuity with meaning.

That's the dream."

Uncle folded his newspaper. "Then you're not as rebellious as you sound."

"And you're not as old-school as you think."

They both laughed, the first treaty between two centuries.

Between Stops

The train curved; she lost balance; I steadied her elbow. No violins, just the hum of motion, her perfume briefly overruling Delhi.

"Thanks," she said, settling back.

"First rescue of the day. Call it a restore point."

"Planning more?"

"Depends on metro traffic and your future balance issues."

She smiled, just slightly. That almost-smile, the one that forgives you for everything and nothing.

Unfiltered

"Want to hear my real problem?" she asked.

"Always."

"My biodata turns me into a product, height, salary, complexion, cooking. All columns, no truth."

I nodded. "My version makes me a punchline, poha, sarcasm, unresolved childhood trauma. Not optimised at all."

"At least yours is funny."

"And yours?"

"Optimised for approval," she said. "Perfect font, polite hobbies, safe answers. Looks neat. Feels fake."

"Because there's no room to be wrong?"

She met my eyes. "Because there's no room to be human."

The train rattled. Even Delhi seemed to hold its breath.

Honest Confessions

"So," I asked, "what scares you most about love?"

You first."

"Settling for less, just to look settled. Losing myself for stability points."

She nodded slowly. "Write mine too."

"Being trapped in someone else's idea of a good life?"
"Exactly. I don't want a 'forever' that feels like pause."
The crowd thinned; our reflections merged in the glass, two faces overlapping, unsure which side of the line they belonged to.

The Platform Pause

Her stop approached. She stood.
"Same time tomorrow?" I asked.
"Same train," she said, pretending it was routine, not ritual.
She paused at the door. "By the way, you talk too much." "Occupational hazard. Founders pitch even without funding."
She shook her head, smiling. "See you, Aarav with two A's."
The doors slid shut.
My reflection in the glass grinned back, like it knew something I didn't.

Rhea's Reflection

That night, she dropped her bag and sank onto the bed. Phone buzzing, client mails, Simran's memes, life on autopilot. She ignored them all.
The metro replayed, crowd, noise, laughter, and one man who understood her silence without a translation.

Not perfect. Just real.

She had spent years perfecting control, career, timelines, expectations checked off like calendar events. But this? This was gloriously unplanned.

Maybe unpredictability is the first sign of being alive.

She opened her planner, drew a small circle on tomorrow's date, and wrote three words beside it: Same train. Maybe.

Closing Montage

Some meetings are accidents. Others are algorithms pretending to be fate.

Maybe destiny books the ticket, the app just assigns the seat, and sometimes, you sit beside the one person who will rewrite your Wi-Fi password, and your life.

Chapter 6

The Project from Hell

When the PowerPoint dies,
chemistry boots up.

My laptop **wheezed like an underpaid intern**. The client's 10:00 a.m. deadline blinked red, a corporate "sharp" time, which always means everyone arrives dull.

Arrival

9:45 a.m. Gurugram. The glass doors of BluePeak Ventures hissed open like opportunity testing its brakes, all chrome, glass, and sharp ambition. Even the air inside smelled of espresso and expectation.
I tugged at my collar. My laptop bag felt heavier than usual, perhaps with the weight of rent, salaries, and three unpaid invoices disguised as optimism.

Pranav's voice looped in my head: "Chill bro, small demo, easy money." I should've known: no sentence beginning with *chill bro* ever ends well.

This wasn't just a meeting. It was oxygen disguised as funding.

Inside, a glass-walled conference room waited: twelve chairs, one projector, and a large man tapping a *Montblanc* like it ran on caffeine, the investor.

The client sat at the head of the glass table, pen tapping a death march. My shoulder ached from the laptop strap.

Then the door slid open.

Rhea walked in.

Her boss followed, phone in hand, trailed by an intern balancing files and destiny.

Recognition hit like déjà vu with better lighting. She stopped mid-step. I forgot how to move.

For half a second, professionalism held its breath.

"You two know each other?" the client asked.

Rhea blinked once, recovery flawless. "Briefly," she said.

"Long story," I added.

Her boss coughed. The intern pretended to find life purpose in PowerPoint.

I blinked. "You're with BluePeak?"

"I'm with BrandArch Agency," she said, recovering fast. "We handle their re-launch strategy." Pause. "You?"

"Product side. Tech partner."

"Perfect," the client smiled. "You'll coordinate well. **One plan. No drama."**

Our mutual smile said the same thing: *Of course. Because the universe loves irony.*

The Setup

Rhea whispered, "Please tell me your demo works."

"It worked at home," I said. "Like democracy."

Her team set up their laptop. Rhea's slides began: clean visuals, calm tone, clear, precise.

"Consumer pain point... hero message... conversion flow..."

Click. Click. Click.

Then, black.

The projector coughed, flickered, and died dramatically.

Black screen. Panic. Silence

The investor's pen stopped tapping.

"Minor tech issue with port," Rhea said smoothly, switching tone from panic to poise. "We'll be live in a minute."

The client smiled the way executioners smile before formality. "This is your big idea?"

Her jaw tightened.

"I can fix it," I whispered.

"Stick to product," she said through her teeth.

"The product's dying with the projector," I whispered back.

"Clients hate chaos."

"Clients hate silence more."

She didn't reply, but didn't stop me either.

I unplugged their HDMI, connected mine. My laptop fan rose like a temple chant. The screen flickered back to life, crooked, dim, but alive. The BluePeak logo appeared.

Rhea exhaled. The client lowered his weaponized pen.

The Pitch

She stepped forward, calm as ever.

"BluePeak Ventures isn't just funding ideas. It's investing in **experiences**."

Investor: "And the product experience?"

I took cue. "Seamless. One-tap onboarding, zero friction. We built it to behave like intuition, not software."

She added, "Exactly why we positioned it as 'Technology that remembers you before you remember passwords.'"

Investor smiled, intrigued. "Show me."

I clicked. "Demo live. Here's your user journey."

Rhea: "First, curiosity, our ad hooks through emotion."
Aarav: "Then function, our interface closes the gap between interest and action."
Rhea: "Three taps to clarity."
Aarav: "Two taps if caffeine is strong."
The room chuckled.
Rhea rode it. "BluePeak wants human connection at digital speed; we coded that in."
Investor leaned back, watching the rhythm, two voices ping-ponging ideas without overlap. She shifted slides; I timed demos. Her metaphors landed, my metrics backed them.
It felt like **jazz in PowerPoint**, improvised, tight, alive.
Lastly, she said, "That's the **why**."
I finished, "And this is the **how**."
Final slide lit the wall.
Silence.
Fifteen minutes of seamless code-switching between business and belief. By the time the intern revived their laptop, the room had already changed temperature.
The client set his pen down. "That," he said, "was seamless."
Then, applause, light, but genuine.
Investor smiled, rare species sighting. "Well done. Let's talk next steps."

Rhea's shoulders dropped half an inch, the universal unit of relief. Mine matched.

Chai at 12:07 p.m.

The office pantry brewed punishment disguised as tea. Only one cup remained, the sacred final pour. Naturally, we both reached.

The office boy split it into two. Adults need small ceremonies to feel alive.

We clinked paper cups.

Through the glass wall, Gurugram traffic pulsed below like an ECG.

She sipped. "You improvise well."

"Survival first, metrics later."

"Good deck," I said. "Your why bought my how time to breathe."

"Good demo," she said. "Your how stopped my why from becoming poetry."

For the first time, work didn't feel like labour, it felt like rhythm. The silence was comfortable. Even the clock stopped judging us.

Then her phone buzzed. She typed something fast.

"Fire?" I asked.

"Small one. I'll put it out."

She smiled, the kind of professional confidence that keeps whole teams from melting down.

Evening Debrief

Afternoon heat pressed against the glass. The client wanted a **same day revised pack**. Of course he did.

We set up camp, Rhea on copy and flow, me on data and code. Our reflections merged on the screen, two faces lit by the same deadline.

"Colour palette?" she asked.

"Not blue. Everyone paints trust blue."

"Warm navy, hint of orange?"

"Perfect. Says ambition without arrogance."

She typed, I adjusted graphs. We didn't flirt. We synced. And that's rarer.

At 6:40 p.m., she hit send.

At 6:45, the client replied**: Perfect, lock it.**

Two words that cancel three days of heartburn.

We slumped back and laughed, the relieved, exhausted laugh of people who'd cheated disaster.

Exit Music

The lift mirror was merciless.

"Your face says peace lost the negotiation," she said.

"Fair. You look like you just signed a **ceasefire**."

The doors opened to a purple-gold sky. Gurugram pretending to be Mediterranean.

She walked out first.

"Coffee?" she asked without turning.

"Only if it's stronger than diplomacy."

Her laugh echoed down the corridor, tired, genuine, enough.

At the gate, a stray dog stretched and yawned. We said hi in unison. It ignored us with grace.

"Tomorrow?" she asked.

"Same train?"

"Depends if I sleep."

Delhi wind carried the promise of rain.

Rain & Tea

The drizzle started as we reached the chai stall near the gate. Two glasses, two shoulders nearly touching.

"Today was good," she said, half-testing the thought.

"We were better together than polite apart."

"Don't get poetic," she warned.

"Occupational hazard."

She smiled, professional, almost personal. "Good. Let's keep the momentum."

Rain pinged on tin, cardamom filled the air, and the world paused long enough for something wordless to grow.

When she left, her auto's taillight blinked like a heartbeat disappearing into traffic.

Some partnerships begin before the people involved realise it. And some victories don't add to revenue, they just remind you you're not building alone.

Not a grand beginning. Just two heartbeats finding the same rhythm in the noise.

Chapter 7

Brothers, Sisters & the Love Guru

Every hero needs a sidekick with bad timing and better advice.

The Mehta Household: Post-Mortem

Dinner at the Mehtas' is not a meal; it's a live sitcom that refuses to end. Three episodes nightly. No commercials. The table overflows with steel bowls, opinions, and unsolicited advice.

Pranav twirled his roti like a mic. "So, Mr. Start-up," he said, "when are we announcing the merger with Miss PowerPoint? I hear the stock is performing well."

"I'm not merging," I said. "We're just collaborating, limited period, renewable clause."

Aditi laughed into her dal. "You co-presented, you co-blushed, you co-survived a projector failure. Admit it."

Maa's radar beeped. "Who is this? Is she the one from Shaadi.com?" "No one," I said too fast.

"Ah," Pranav nodded solemnly. "The famous Delhi girl, Miss No One. High-priority stealth mode."

Aditi raised her spoon like a toast.

"Love-Guru Rule #21: When a man says 'no one,' it's usually everyone."

Dad hid behind his newspaper, the Switzerland of the family.

Maa smiled like an ambush. "She sounds cultured."

"She sounds real," Pranav said, enjoying himself. "And if she survived Aarav, she deserves a gallantry award."

"Big talk," I said. "You proposed with a Paytm cashback notification."

Aditi beamed. "Best ROI of his life."

Pranav grinned. "At least I didn't spill coffee as foreplay."

Later, on the balcony, the city glowed orange through a haze of nostalgia and pollution.

Pranav leaned against the railing, equal parts elder brother and TED Talk.

"So," he said, "still pretending it's just professional admiration?"

"Yes, I like her, you were right, but do we have to replay this episode again?"

"You sound like you're managing a project, not confessing feelings."

"She's smarter than me."

He smirked. "Exactly. That's why you look terrified instead of in love."

"I'm just being careful."

"Careful is good for contracts," he said. "Not for people."

I looked out at the traffic lights blinking below us. "You sound like Dad."

"Yeah," he said, grinning. "But with better hair and no fixed deposits."

I laughed, the kind that escaped before logic could stop it.

Pranav clapped my shoulder. "There it is, the proof. You're gone."

I didn't deny it this time.

"Humility unlocked. Marriage material confirmed."

Aditi appeared with kulfi, the official dessert of sibling interventions.

"Stop pitching. Try honesty, it's rarer. Treat her like a person, not an investor."

Pranav added, "And make sure next time, the projector works with her laptop. Symbolism matters."

Pranav finished his kulfi and leaned in, adopting his most profound Guru voice.

> *"Love Guru Rule #12: Real chemistry doesn't need violins. It shows up in PowerPoint."*

Aditi snorted. "You should trademark your nonsense."

He turned to me. "Listen, Aarav. When two people start finishing sentences mid-slide, something bigger than Wi-Fi is syncing."

I smiled despite myself. "You're impossible."

"That's what married wisdom sounds like. You'll see someday."

Aditi nudged him. "He's right, though. I've seen your chaos after bad meetings. Today, you look... peaceful."

"Because the pitch went well."

"Or because someone made it better."

Aditi smiled. "Say thank you to the girl who saved you."

"I did."

"Say it again tomorrow," she said. "Even if she doesn't need it."

Pranav winked. "And don't forget, love is just collaboration with better music."

"Blocked," I said, grinning into the cushion. Downstairs, Maa hummed old Kishore songs.

The Sharma Home: Stability & Small Chaos

Rhea's world ran on clockwork , her younger sister, Simran, ran on chaos and coffee.

Mr. Sharma scrolled stock updates. Mrs. Sharma scrolled potential sons-in-law. Simran scrolled reels. The holy trinity of distraction.

"So," Mrs. Sharma began, "that boy from the meeting, nice family?

Stable hours?"

"Colleague, Maa. Same project," Rhea said.

"Still, good manners," Mrs. Sharma said. "He saved your presentation."

"By fixing the projector?" Rhea said.

"Exactly," Simran chimed in. "He's your debugging tool."

Rhea threw a cushion. Simran ducked, grinning. "He's cute though. Bit awkward. I like awkward, it's honest. They haven't optimised their social profile yet."

"You like Wi-Fi passwords," Rhea said.

Translation: you like things that are dependable, accessible, and secure once connected.

Simran clutched her heart. "Elder-sister burn! Somebody pass aloe vera and validation!"

Mr. Sharma didn't look up. "If you're dating, make sure he pays taxes. And his company has P&L; clarity."

"Papa!" both daughters protested.

"Just saying. Stability matters."

"Love matters," Simran countered.

"Both would be nice," Rhea murmured.

Mrs. Sharma softened. "We only want you happy, beta. The final product must be perfect."

Rhea smiled faintly. "Happiness doesn't come with an OTP, Maa."

Simran leaned closer. "So, Miss Workaholic, any cute chaos at work today?"

"Some," Rhea said. "**Half-cup-of-chai kind, small but warm**."

She watched her sister longer than the joke required. "People wait for grand chemistry," she said. "**Most just need someone who doesn't flinch when we're ordinary**."

Rhea threw the cushion again, but her smile stayed.

Parallel Nights: The Unspoken Sync

Aarav

Laptop open, glow flickering on my face.

I typed into Notes: Things to fix: pitch, perspective.

I stared at the second word. Maybe it wasn't the work that needed realignment.

That night, as I updated our progress sheet, one line stood out: Collaborated with external agency, unexpected synergy. I didn't write her name. Didn't

need to. Some victories don't add to revenue, they just remind you you're not building alone.
After a pause, I added: Maybe text her.
My thumb hovered long enough for the screen to dim. I didn't.

Rhea

Her home glowed with half-lit rooms and half-finished thoughts. Simran's playlist hummed softly through the wall.
Rhea took a screenshot of the email, "**Perfect, lock it**", not for proof, for joy. She thought of a dead projector, a silent room, and a boy who didn't ask before helping, he just helped. No grand gestures. Just teamwork that worked.
At her desk, planner open like a confession.
She wrote: Morning review – 9:30 a.m. (joint). Then, smaller, almost shy: Carry sugar packets.
She smiled. It wasn't about tea. It was about remembering, the small things that stay sweet, even when unsaid. Outside, Delhi blinked through its insomnia, horns, dogs, and late-night chai. Two people, two laptops, one unspoken conversation.

Closing Beat

Pranav's voice note arrived late.

"Love-Guru Rule #22: When the universe keeps putting you in the same frame, stop cropping the picture. Accept the full aspect ratio."

Somewhere across the city, Rhea's phone pinged at the same moment. She smiled, not knowing why.

Night air drifted through the balcony, carrying Delhi's hum and a half-remembered tune. Rhea stood by the window, mug in hand, staring at the restless skyline. She thought of her father's caution, her sister's jokes, her own calm in a room full of chaos. And of one boy who turned that noise into quiet.

Outside, a metro roared past, windows glowing like a moving constellation. Inside, she allowed herself a longer pause, no promises, just possibilities.

Some nights don't need endings; they just need a reason to begin again.

Chapter 8

Finding Rhythm in the Garba Chaos

Destiny staged a meet-cute

The Invitation No One Planned

Delhi nights in October carry their own mischief, cool air, loud lights, and festivals competing for attention.

Pranav and Aditi had dragged me to a Navratri mela at Dilli Haat.

"Cultural enrichment," Aditi said.

"Free snacks," Pranav corrected.

The ground pulsed with dhols, fairy lights, and aunties armed with dandiyas like precision weapons.

Somewhere between stalls of chaat and overpriced terracotta lamps, I started regretting life choices.
"Relax," Pranav said. "Garba is cardio disguised as community."
"I don't do group projects," I muttered.
"You did one with Rhea," he shot back.
I ignored him, until the DJ announced, "Next round." That's when I saw her.
Rhea. White-and-gold lehenga, hair braided with tiny flowers, cheeks already streaked with colour. She was laughing with Simran near the juice counter.
The universe, clearly, had no chill.

The Collision Course

Simran spotted me first. Her grin widened like she'd found a trailer worth gossiping about.
"Well, if it isn't Mr Pitch-Perfect," she said.
Rhea turned, and the smile froze halfway.
"Aarav," she said, surprised but not displeased.
"Delhi's smaller than it claims," I replied.
Simran excused herself, conveniently. "I'll go pray to the goddess of timing."
We stood there, music swirling, people spinning in circles around us.
"So, you do attend cultural events," she teased.
"Only when blackmailed by family."
"Figures."

The DJ yelled, "Everyone join!" Before logic could object, someone shoved a pair of dandiyas into my hands.

Rhea smirked. "Come on, start-up boy. Let's see you handle real coordination."

The Dance Disaster

Garba looks easy until you try it with the wrong rhythm and the right person.

I spun left; she spun right; a stick flew.

"Watch it!" she laughed.

"I'm beta-testing my coordination," I said.

"Failing the update," she shot back.

I moved like a Wi-Fi signal, unstable, delayed, mostly guessing.

"Left, right, rotate!" she shouted.

"I'm innovating. Asymmetrical dance form," I said.

"Injury innovation?"

"User-tested. Limited success."

Soon we were laughing too much to care. The circle around us blurred, drums, colours, chaos, and in the middle of it, something felt... easy again.

Her movements were graceful, mine were accidental poetry, but somehow the rhythm caught up. We danced until the song ended, breathless, laughing, cheeks dusted red.

People clapped. One aunty shouted, "Good jodi!"

Rhea rolled her eyes. "Delhi aunties ship faster than Amazon."

I grinned. "Maybe they're just observant."

The Teasing Afterglow

We found a corner near the food stalls. The air smelled of jalebis and wet earth.

"So, haunting me now?" she asked, mock-serious.

"Pure coincidence. The universe runs on your schedule."

"Then remind the universe I'm off duty today."

We shared a plate of papdi chaat, both pretending not to notice how her fingers brushed mine when she passed the spoon.

Her head tilting back, the sound bright enough to drown the dhols.

"*I forgot how easy it is to talk to you*," she admitted.

"Maybe that's the problem," I said.

She gave me a look. "And what's the solution?"

"Keep talking."

The Rain Interlude

Delhi weather, forever dramatic, decided to join in. A light drizzle sprinkled over the fairground; people scattered under tents. Rhea and I stayed where we were.

"Deja vu," she said.

"Except no fireworks, no microphone, just rain again."

"Rain and you," she said softly.

I smiled. "Reliable combo."

The drizzle deepened into laughter and chaos. We ran to the shade of a banyan stall, soaked but grinning.

Her dupatta stuck to her cheek; I brushed it back. She didn't move away.

"Every festival," I said, "you show up like a plot twist."

"Maybe you just keep reading the same story."

"Maybe it's worth rereading."

The Unplanned Goodbye

When the rain thinned, the crowd began to leave.

Simran waved from the exit. "Uber's waiting!"

Rhea turned to me. "Walk me till the gate?"

"Always."

We wove through puddles and fairy-light reflections.

"I'll admit," she said, "you made Garba less terrible."

"And you made it survivable."

"So, what next?"

"Another accidental meeting?" I offered. She smiled. *"Or maybe an intentional one."*

She got into the cab, window half-down.

"Goodnight, Aarav."

"Night, Rhea."

The car rolled away, tyres rippling through the puddles. For once, I didn't chase or analyse or overthink. I just stood there, drenched, smiling at the rain that kept finding new excuses to bring us together.

Closing Beat

Later that night, I texted:

Aarav: So, when's the next cultural enrichment?

Rhea: When you learn basic Garba rhythm.

Aarav: Never, then.

Rhea: Perfect. Some things shouldn't change.

I laughed into the dark.

Maybe some dances aren't about steps, they're about staying long enough to find the same beat.

Not a cliff-hanger, just a handrail they're both holding. Love's not building speed; it's learning balance.

Chapter 9

In Metro

Two stops, one heartbeat, and a circle drawn on fogged glass.

Monday Morning Blues

Fairy lights gone; only fluorescents stayed faithful.
The metro slid in with its usual sigh, doors opening like resignation and hope sharing the same seat.
Delhi had gone back to deadlines. Garba glitter had turned into inbox glow.
I stepped in, half-awake, half-alive.
Our start-up app finally had users now, small number, big hope. Every notification felt like a heartbeat we couldn't afford to lose. Some mornings, I couldn't tell if I was running a company or just running on caffeine and denial.
Two stops later, she entered. Rhea, earphones, tote, that I-run-on-purpose face.

We nodded, the wordless greeting that says: So, we're still doing this.
Somehow that small nod steadied the day more than caffeine ever could.

The Familiar Banter

"Recovered from your heroic Garba performance?" she asked, pulling one earphone down.
"Barely."
She laughed, soft and unguarded. The sound filled the coach better than air-conditioning.
"Breakfast?" she asked.
"Bread, hope, one samosa." "Balanced diet, complex carbs and anxiety."
"You?" "Poha. Made by Dad. With extra peanuts of rebellion."
"Love disguised as cholesterol." "Precisely."
That gentle rhythm between us returned, half teasing, half remembering.
In that softness lives something dangerous: the comfort of repetition.
The mind starts calling it belonging long before the heart agrees.

Professional Pulse

The coach swayed; she steadied herself on the pole beside me.
"Big meeting today?" she asked.

"Maybe the one that decides if my start-up dies gracefully."
"Need good luck?" "Always. We're running on prayers and chai."
She drew a tiny circle in the fogged window with her finger. "Done. You're insured."
"You believe in that?"
"I believe in people trying. And the power of a clean circle."
"Then I'm covered. If the analyst asks for proof, I'll show him the window."
She smiled, quiet, approving. For a second I believed the circle might hold our names somewhere, invisible but safe.

The Crowd and the Calm

A vendor yelled, "Power bank! Keychain! Love symbol! Buy one for your crush!"
Rhea raised a brow. "See? Delhi sells everything, even metaphors."
"Should we buy one?"
"What, love or power bank?"
"Whichever lasts longer."
"Try me," she said, half-teasing, half-serious.
The air changed. Chai to espresso.
Some answers are meant to stay suspended; certainty might ruin them.

The Pause Between Stations

At Central Secretariat, the crowd thinned. We found two empty seats, a miracle rarer than sincerity in LinkedIn posts.

"Do you think about next year?" she asked, head tipped back against the window.

"Mostly in tax terms and runway extension."

"No, life-wise. Where you'll be."

"Fewer unpaid bills. Maybe a coffee place that knows my order." "Simple dream."

"Yours?"

She hesitated. "Somewhere I can breathe. With someone who gets my silence. Someone who knows the difference between a pause and a full stop."

"That's oddly specific. Narrowing your search parameters." "Maybe I've started narrowing my search."

The tracks blurred, silver ribbons of motion.

Our reflections overlapped in the glass, two faces that looked *like a maybe* learning to trust itself.

Shared Confession

She spoke again, softer.

"Do you ever get scared that everything you're building could fall apart overnight? Career, relationship, everything?"

"All the time," I said. "That's why I keep joking. Cheaper than therapy."

"Same," she said. "Smiling is my firewall."
We laughed, not to fix anything, just to breathe through the truth.

Departure and Memory

Her station arrived. She stood, adjusted her scarf.
"Tomorrow, same time?" "Same coach," I said. "I'll save you a seat."
"Save me a coffee instead. I'll make sure your pitch is good." "Both. Bundle offer."
"Ambitious."
"Occupational hazard."
The doors slid open.
She hesitated a heartbeat, then mouthed, *See you*. It sounded ordinary. It felt like a plan the heart had already signed.

Rhea's Reflection

That night she opened her planner. Tomorrow - client call 9 a.m.
Below it she wrote: Train - 9 a.m. (our seat) and drew a small circle, the same one she'd traced on the fogged window.
Inside that circle lived unspoken hopes: that he keeps showing up, that she won't have to pretend control forever,
that maybe, just maybe, this ordinary commute is the start of something worth missing.

She closed the planner carefully, as if sealing a secret.

The phone buzzed : Simran.

"Still fighting the world or just one man this time?" she asked.

Rhea sighed. "Neither. Just learning silence."

"Careful," Simran said. "Silence is addictive. You start mistaking it for peace."

Rhea smiled faintly. "Maybe peace is all I have energy for."

"Then find someone who gives you that without muting you," Simran replied.

The call ended, but the words lingered like background music, low, insistent, impossible to ignore.

Closing Beat

Sometimes someone becomes part of your life so naturally that your fears and hopes start learning to live together,

like two metro tracks, side by side, unsure of the destination but moving in the same direction.

Not every love story needs a grand stage.

Chapter 10

The Almost Confession

Between rain and restraint, love rehearses its first draft.

The Sky Between Yes and No

The sky looked like half-finished watercolour , smudged blue, undecided. The kind of sky that can't choose rain or restraint. Maybe that was us , carrying too much that never fully spills.

Rhea texted first.

Rhea: *Coffee break? Human contact required. Emotional bandwidth low.*

Me: *Approved*. The usual? Ready for deployment.

Rhea: *Approved*, with sarcasm shot on top.

The Usual Place

The café behind her office was small enough to keep secrets, loud enough to disguise them. Our neutral ground.

She was already there, white shirt, loose bun escaping discipline. Her eyes flicked up, softened just enough to make breathing a conscious act.

"On time," she said.

"I'm trying punctuality. New rebellion."

"Dangerous. You might lose your chalta hai charm."

"Don't worry. I plan a relapse."

Her laugh cracked halfway, like a file still buffering.

"Rough day?" I asked. She stirred her drink. "Just ... human contact required."

"Mission accomplished."

For a while we just existed , two caffeine molecules holding each other's temperature.

Half Conversations

We talked traffic, politics nobody understood, clients who demanded miracles on retainer. Words skimmed the surface while something quieter trembled underneath.

"You ever think we meet too often?" she asked.

"Depends. Are we measuring in guilt or joy?"

"Both." "Then not enough."

Her spoon froze mid-stir.

A smile began, faint, cautious, like hope testing its voice. She didn't answer. She didn't need to.

Outside, the sky finally surrendered.
Rain began the way feelings do, hesitant, then sudden.

The Power Cut

Thunder, and darkness.
The café blinked out for two seconds, long enough to reveal everything.
One candle, one heartbeat, one terrible idea called honesty.
"You're staring," she whispered.
"Research. Trying to understand why time stops."
"Find anything?" "Still collecting data."
The lights came back too soon, like reality barging into a private moment still taking notes.

The Run in the Rain

We left together, rain chasing us out.
We ran to the metro, drenched and laughing, the kind of laughter that hides a hundred confessions.
Her hair clung to her face; my shirt to my skin. We didn't care.
"Remind me why we live here?" she panted.
"Because no other city offers samosas at 2 a.m."
"And heartbreak at 2 p.m."
"Occupational hazard."
We laughed again, lighter this time, until silence arrived dressed as breathlessness.

Under the Roof

At the station roof, she wrung water from her sleeves. The air smelled of wet concrete and maybe.

"Rhea, if I ever start saying stupid things, "

"You already do."

"No, emotional stupid."

She looked straight at me. "Go on."

"I'd want you to listen anyway."

Something flickered in her eyes, half fear, half yes.

"And if I said something emotionally stupid?" she asked.

"I'd probably write about it. Pretend it was fiction."

"Good. Then we'll both be safe."

Safe, the cruellest word when two people are this close to falling.

The Metro Ride

We found seats facing each other. Her eyes held mine too long, long enough to say what lips couldn't risk.

"Your eyes do this thing," she murmured.

"What thing?" "They look like they're about to confess and then change their mind."

"Occupational hazard," I said.

"Keep it that way. The mystery suits you."

The train hissed to a stop , her station. Neither of us moved.

Finally, she stood.

"Tomorrow?" I asked.
She nodded. "Tomorrow."
Then, almost too quiet for the train to hear:
"Aarav ... don't overthink this. Just be here."
And she was gone.

Rhea's Reflection

Later, she towel-dried her hair and sat by the window. Rain still whispered outside.
Her planner lay open. Tomorrow , client call 10 a.m.
Beneath it she wrote: Train - 9 a.m. (our seat) Then, after a pause: I think he feels it too.
She closed the book before the ink dried. Inside her chest, something was opening , and that terrified her more than losing it.
Some almost-confessions are louder than love. Sometimes not saying it is how you say it best.

Chapter 11

Diwali Dinner Disaster

Fireworks outside; emotional combustion within.

The Invitation That Should've Been an Email

It started with Pranav, always the matchmaker disguised as comic relief.

"Family dinner. Rhea's family too. Real-world LinkedIn."

Maa's eyes gleamed. "Yes! Let's make it joint pooja. Prosperity doubles when families connect."

I froze mid-bite. "Maybe not this Diwali, "

She'd already sent the WhatsApp invite.

Aditi patted my shoulder. "Relax. It's food, not an alliance meeting." She'd regret that optimism later.

Arrival & Auspicious Chaos

The house looked like it had overdosed on fairy lights.

Pranav supervised laddoos, Aditi arranged diyas, Chachi showered blessings; the neighbour, as always, RSVP'd without invitation.

Doorbell.

Rhea stood there, gold kurta, hair loose, smile tight.

Behind her, Mr and Mrs Sharma radiated polite tension.

Our eyes met. Hers said brace yourself. Mine said already doing that.

"Welcome, welcome!" Maa sang. "Aarav, light diyas together, auspicious for new beginnings."

Chachi added, "Yes, perfect couple! Verified match!"

Pranav whispered, "Festival of lights, not matchmaking."

Aditi whispered back, "Let them finish the episode."

Dinner Table Diplomacy

The table shimmered, silver bowls, ghee, ambition.

Maa opened the pitch: "Rhea beta works in marketing, very creative!"

"Yes," Rhea smiled. "Brand strategy."

Mr Sharma nodded. "Good. As long as clients pay on time. Stability matters."

Aditi laughed lightly. "In this market, even stability's on subscription."

Mild laughter, except Mr Sharma, who recalculated his approval rating.

Maa turned proudly. "Our Aarav too, entrepreneur spirit, big plans."

Mr Sharma: "Good-good. Stability matters."

I smiled, pretending start-ups and stability had ever met.

He leaned forward. "Series A secured?"

Maa jumped in. "He has vision!"

Mrs Sharma's polite smile translated to: vision doesn't pay EMI.

She added, "Rhea also works hard. Maybe she'll steady him, be the anchor."

Pranav: "Steadying Aarav is a full-time job. We pay emotional salary."

Laughter. Temporary relief.

Tradition Triggers

Between refills of paneer and pride, Chachi declared,

"In our family, daughters-in-law make the first sweet for pooja. Good omen."

Maa sparkled. "Yes! Tomorrow, Rhea can try!"

Rhea smiled, civil. "Aunty, I burn toast. My culinary skills are minimal."

Chachi giggled. "Practice! After marriage, she'll learn."

Rhea's father chuckled. "We're not in a hurry. Her career's priority."

Silence stretched, thin and dangerous.

Aditi attempted diplomacy. "Times change, gender equality, shared load."

Mr Sharma replied calmly, "Equality is good, beta, till bills start arriving. Responsibilities must balance."

The tone was common sense; the subtext, centuries old.

Rhea's eyes met mine: *Will you say something*?

My lips chose neutrality.

The First Crack

Maa tried a rescue smile. "Ambition is fine, beta, but women balance homes naturally. It's their gift."

Rhea's jaw tightened. "Balance is teamwork, Aunty. Takes two committed co-founders."

Mr Sharma added, "Of course. But men need support, not competition."

Competition landed like a slap we pretended not to hear.

Aditi's spoon paused. Pranav's joke died half-born.

Rhea said quietly, "Partnership isn't competition. It's shared wins. If one must lose for the other to feel secure, that's not marriage, it's a race."

No one answered. Outside, a cracker exploded, too on cue.

Balcony Truths

Dinner ended. The air thinned with politeness. Rhea escaped to the balcony. I followed.

"Sorry," I began. "They didn't mean, "

"They did," she said. Not angry, tired. "Legacy software."

"Then explain it to them. You translate investor decks daily."

"I didn't want to make it worse."

"Sometimes silence is worse. It reads like agreement."

Pranav called from inside, "Aarav! Pooja time!" I stayed rooted.

She looked away. "Go," she said. "It's your family's show."

She walked in first; I followed like a bad echo.

The Aarti That Didn't Heal

Maa handed her the diya. "Beta, hold it with Aarav, unity symbol."

"Of course," Rhea said, brittle, polite.

We circled the flame together. Her fingers brushed mine, steady, cold. She sang the aarti perfectly. I forgot the words halfway.

Chachi whispered, "After wedding, this will be your role every year!"

Rhea finished the verse and stepped back.

Family photo time, Chachi called out, "Rhea beta, come, stand here"

"No, Aunty," she said softly. "Tonight, I'd rather stand with my parents."

Flash. Camera. Click. Sounded exactly like a door shutting.

Departure & Debrief

After they left, silence hung heavier than smoke.

Pranav: "You froze at the worst moment."

Aditi: "She wanted empathy, not etiquette. You chose the wrong side."

Maa: "We were just talking! I was giving guidance!"

Pranav: "Talking wasn't the problem, Maa. Listening was."

Later, balcony. Incense fading. My phone buzzed.

Rhea: Thanks for the evening.

I stared.

Me: For surviving it? Blinking dots. Then nothing.

Seconds later, Rhea: "**I thought you saw me**."

Four words. Soft. Unbearable.

I typed I'm sorry. Too small.

Typed I did see you. Too late.

Left the phone face-down. Her message still burned behind my eyes.

She hadn't meant *looked at me*. She'd meant *understood me*. Chose me.

I hadn't.

Rhea's Night

Back home, she dropped her dupatta on the chair, switched off the lights, sat in the dark.

Down the hall, her parents discussed nice family, well-spoken boy, needs time.

She let them fade.

She replayed the dinner, Chachi's giggle, her father's pride as judgment, ***Aarav's silence***.

"I wasn't asking him to fight," she whispered. "*Just to see me.*"

Anger passes. Disappointment stays.

She turned her phone over; his name glowed unanswered.

She exhaled, slow. "Coward."

Then she wrote in her planner: Tomorrow, breathe. Expect clarity, not apology.

Outside, leftover rockets screamed and died before they could bloom.

Some nights don't explode. They fade , quietly taking something with them.

Closing Beat

I sat until the sky dulled to smoke. Maa called, "Aarav, sweets for neighbours! Social obligation phase two!"

"Coming," I answered. My voice didn't sound like mine.

In the reflection of the balcony glass, I could still read her text: "*I thought you saw me*".
Some love stories don't break with noise. They break when silence finally learns to speak.
Not a blast, just the long *phut* of two hearts out of sync.

Chapter 12

Silent Metro Ride

Sometimes the loudest argument is the one nobody speaks.

The Morning After

Morning arrived like a screen dimmed, not switched off. Delhi looked the same, vendors shouting fresh!, autos negotiating physics , but everything moved half a step slower, as if the city itself had a hangover from celebration.

The air tasted faintly of burnt paper. Rangolis had smudged into pastel ghosts outside shuttered shops. Someone had forgotten to take down a string of fairy lights; it blinked like an exhausted heartbeat.

I reached the platform early and stood where we always stood, third pillar from the stairway, under the speaker that mispronounces stations.

My phone still glowed with her message even when the screen was black.
"I thought you saw me."
The quietest, most brutal bug-report I'd ever received.
The Train Arrives
A non-stop train thundered through, wind slapping my shirt flat against my ribs. It felt deserved.
The 9:02 slid in with its usual sigh, doors opening to the choreography of push, squeeze.
I stepped inside, found my corner near the door. Breath fogged the cold glass, then vanished , like intention.
Two stations later, she entered. Rhea.
Hair tied back, kajal a shade darker, mouth fixed in that already-decided-to-be-fine line.
She scanned the coach, saw me, and gave the smallest nod, a courtesy, and only that. The kind that says: We are civilised people. We will behave.
I lifted a hand halfway, then dropped it before it could become wave or want.
The crowd carried her to the opposite handrail. Two feet , and a lifetime , between us.

Parallel Silence

Metal groaned; a shopping bag crinkled like a crushed apology. I risked a glance.

She wasn't looking at me. She watched our reflections break and reform against tunnel lights , light, dark, light, dark , as if counting how long shadows last.

A child near the door began a thin Diwali tune before his mother hushed him. Rhea's eyes softened , a micro-degree of warmth I'd learned to notice , then blinked it away.

At Mandi House, two seats opened across the aisle like a dare.

We both stepped forward , then both stepped back.

A man took one; an aunty with glass bangles claimed the other.

Unsaid Words

The recorded voice announced Next station, Central Secretariat. It sounded practised, not kind.

"Coffee?" I said finally , a peace flag on a toothpick.

She turned; for a half-second the old warmth returned, like a visitor who still knew the door code. Then the visitor remembered it wasn't home anymore.

She shook her head.

"Okay," I said. The word arrived with nowhere to sit.

A man selling pens threaded through our silence. "Ten rupees! Smooth writing! Guaranteed flow!" He held one out. I almost bought it, just to give my hand something to do.

Her fingers tightened on the pole; the smallest tremor, like a sentence catching on a word it can't say.

She noticed me noticing, straightened her grip. The message was clear: Don't read me. *Not today.*

Truth in Fragments

"I should've spoken," I said at last.

She kept her eyes on the window.

"Yes."

One syllable. Clean. True. Not cruel.

It hurt more than any argument could have.

The train hissed into another tunnel.

In the glass we stood side by side, almost, the silver band of the handrail slicing the reflection like a horizon:

above it, the parts we show; below it, the parts we don't.

Two schoolgirls squeezed between us, sharing one earbud and a secret.

They laughed into their palms. I envied the simplicity of anything that can be hidden and still survive.

Small Honesties

Her voice came without warning.

"My dad says people become practical with age."

I glanced up. "Maybe practicality is just fear that learned manners."

She nodded faintly. "*Maybe.*"

"I was afraid," I said.

"I know."

Another truth. Another absence of drama.

We were building a quiet city out of honest sentences and calling it survival.

When Politeness Hurts

Rajiv Chowk.

Half the crowd spilled out; half pushed in.

A seat freed next to me. I didn't offer it. She didn't move. Good manners felt vulgar in the wrong moment.

Across the aisle, an uncle folded his newspaper like a judge closing a case.

He looked at us, the universal adult curiosity for the mess young people still call love, then looked away, unimpressed. I envied his boredom.

"Last night," I began. "When you said, "

"I know what I said." Her tone calm, edged. "I meant it.

I needed you to see me. Not as a project partner or your mother's idea of progress. **Me**."

"I do," I said. It came out smaller than belief.

"Then act like it."

Not a stab. A map line drawn clear.

The Handkerchief

We passed an open stretch; sunlight rushed in, turning dust into tiny galaxies.
I reached into my bag, found a handkerchief I never use, and offered it across the crowd, not to fix anything, just because water had gathered at the corner of her eye, not enough to fall, just enough to sting.
She blinked it away before the cotton reached. "Keep it," she said softly. "You might need it more."
We both smiled, the sad kind that knows exactly where it sits on the timeline: between mistake and lesson.

Departures

Her station neared. She shifted her tote to the other shoulder, a motion I'd learned meant leaving soon.
I hated that I knew this and loved that I knew this.
When the chime sounded, she stepped closer, close enough for whatever we were to feel itself one last time.
She didn't touch me.
Her perfume carried jasmine and rain; it reminded me of a balcony we hadn't shared.
"Tomorrow?" I asked. The word felt like a fragile boat in bad weather.
She considered, then spared me the cruelty of false hope.

"I don't know."

The doors opened. She turned, then back again.

"Aarav... learn to speak before the moment ends. It's expensive to replace."

Then she was gone, absorbed by the daily river of purpose and pretence that is our city in motion.

Aftermath

The doors closed. The train moved.

Somewhere above, a delayed cracker cracked the sky; the sound arrived late, like our conversations.

I sat in the seat no one claimed and stared at my reflection. I looked like someone a beat too slow for his own life.

On the glass, a faint smear of last night's smoke still clung to the world outside. The train carved through it without noticing.

I pressed a thumb to the cold and wrote nothing. The fog erased it for me , mercy in small gestures.

Some commutes are measured in stations. This one was measured in all the words we didn't spend in time.

It wasn't a journey through space; it was a journey through silence. Not distance. Just the price of hesitation, paid one station at a time.

Every love story has a silence. This one just arrived on schedule.

Chapter 13

The Suspicious Calls

When data looks like doubt, and love fails two-factor authentication.

The Quiet After Fireworks

The week after Diwali moved like someone had turned down life's volume.

Same metro stations, same office chatter, same messages , just quieter versions of what we used to be.

The connection still existed, but ran on restricted bandwidth.

We still met for coffee.

We still joked.

But something behind her eyes had changed, not anger, but caution, like she'd started handling our conversations **with oven gloves.**

Small Talk, Big Distance

"Hey," I said one morning.

"Hey," she said back.

Silence between us now had shape , polite, efficient, exhausting.

"You free this weekend?" I tried, an outreach disguised as casual.

"Maybe. Big project pitch coming up," she said, checking her phone.

"Big as in career-big or excuse-big?" She looked up.

"Don't start, Aarav. It's real."

I laughed too quickly, as if humour could fix it. It didn't.

Some silences grow teeth.

The Late Calls Begin

It started small.

One missed call at 10:45 p.m. No follow-up. Another night, she replied to my text after two hours: *Sorry, on call.*

At first, I didn't care. Then I did. Then I cared too much.

By midweek, my brain was its own WhatsApp group, full of theories, nonhelpful. Client call? Investor? Ex?

I told myself I had evolved enough not to snoop. Naturally, I started checking her last seen. Integrity test: failed.

Pranav's Clinic for Emotional Hypochondria

Pranav caught me staring at my phone like it owed me closure.

"Still alive?" he asked, chewing peanuts.

"Barely. Running an emotional stress test."

"Work or life?"

"Life."

"Ah," he said. "The one without salary."

He squinted at my screen. "You're checking last seen? Oh no. That's stage-four attachment disorder."

"She's online at midnight. That's... suspicious." "Maybe she's talking to her pillow. It's a better listener."

Aditi walked by with folded laundry. "Leave him. Every man must fight his own ego war once. Rite of passage."

I groaned. "I know she's busy."

"Then believe her," Aditi said.

"What if she's lying?"

Pranav grinned. "Then you'll have content for your heartbreak playlist. Growth."

Half-Conversations

Two days later, we met in the metro canteen.

Rhea looked exhausted, dark circles, messy bun, still beautiful in a way that made logic look stupid.

"Rough week?" I asked.

She nodded. "Investor calls, strategy chaos, 18-hour days. You?"

"Spreadsheets and paranoia."

She smiled faintly. "At least you're honest."

Her phone buzzed. She stepped away, voice brisk: "No, that's not the valuation we discussed... tell Karan we'll revert tomorrow."

Karan. The name hit like a low-frequency alarm.

When she returned: "Sorry. You were saying?"

"I forgot," I lied.

We sat in silence that used to feel comfortable. Now it felt like surveillance.

The Scroll That Hurts More Than Truth

That night, Simran posted a story,

#MidnightCoffee #PowerWomenVibes #PitchLife #KaranSirDeservesBetter

I read it three times. **Karan** Sir. Not boyfriend , worse. Mentor. Legit. Safe. The kind who's always available just enough.

Jealousy doesn't need proof. It just needs imagination and Wi-Fi.

The Call That Broke the Quiet

Saturday, 11:47 p.m. Rain whispering outside. I massaged " Call me, when free".

My phone buzzed. Rhea calling.

"Hey," I said.

"Hey," she answered, distracted. "Can we keep this short? Working."

"Still with Karan?" "Yes.

He wanted revisions for the deck."

"Ah. Karan." The pause that followed was surgical.

"What's that tone?" she asked.

"Nothing. Just observation. He seems... central."

"Because he's my boss." "Convenient."

Her sigh travelled through the line, tired, disappointed, final.

"Aarav, please don't do this. Not you. I need you outside the mistrust protocol."

"I'm not doing anything. Just... noticing patterns."

"Patterns?" "Late calls. Long silences. Data's consistent."

Silence.

Then, softer: "You think I'd lie to you?"

I didn't answer fast enough. That was the mistake.

"Goodnight, Aarav," she said, calm, ending everything without raising her voice.

Not angry. Just gone.

The Misread Sight

Next evening, the city rained again.

I was leaving office when I saw her, outside Café Bloom, white shirt, open hair, laughing with a man in a navy blazer. Tall. Confident. Umbrella guy.

Even from across the road I heard one word, Karan.

I massaged " Hey, can we talk".

My phone buzzed right then: Stuck in meeting. Call later?

I didn't open it. The brain protects pride before love.

System lockout: complete.

The drizzle thickened, blurring logic.

I walked away before reason could explain what emotion had already sentenced.

The Aftermath

At home, I stared at my reflection , not jealous, not furious, just exhausted.

Pranav stepped out for water. "You fought?"

"Define fought."

"Words exchanged?"

"Barely."

"Congratulations," he said. "That's worse."

He clapped my shoulder. "You'll learn. Love dies quietly, like software updates you click later on forever."

Later that night, her message arrived. Everything okay? I didn't reply.

Rhea's Note

Rhea tossed her phone aside, stared at her open planner. Her hair was still damp from the rain.

A drop fell on the page, blurring Investor Call 10 a.m. into Inves... call... am. She smiled sadly. "Even the ink's tired."

She thought of Aarav , not the boy who doubted her, but the one who once made the metro feel lighter.

She whispered to the dark, "I wasn't hiding. I was surviving."

Then she closed the planner, turned off the light.

Love wasn't the problem. Timing was.

Sometimes love doesn't end with goodbye, it just runs out of network.

Two phones lit up that night. Both waited for the other to call first.

Chapter 14

Aarav's Hidden Struggle

Success on paper, failure off-screen.

Morning Lag

Morning light hit the room like an unpaid bill , unwelcome, but inevitable. The ceiling fan groaned, my inbox blinked, and my motivation pressed snooze again.

Subject lines stacked like accusations:

-Payment delayed

-Vendor follow-up urgent

-Reminder: office rent pending

-Investor update call , 4 p.m.

I closed the laptop.

When reality starts sending push notifications, denial becomes the only firewall that still works.

Pretend Calm

Pranav walked in with two mugs.

“Still alive?”

“Barely. Running on fumes and faith.”

He handed me one.

“payment reminder came. Persistent alert.”

“Ok.” “And?”

“I’m thinking. Deploying mitigation strategy.”

He laughed. “Thinking doesn’t pay bills. That’s philosophy, not business.”

“Thanks, Dad.”

“Anytime.”

From the kitchen, Aditi called, “Stop stressing him! His CPU usage is already 100%.”

“Stress is his co-founder,” Pranav said.

They laughed. I didn’t.

The startup was sinking quietly , one unpaid invoice, one delayed client, one fake smile at a time.

The numbers on my spreadsheet looked like a heartbeat losing rhythm.

When Performance Becomes Personality

By noon, Rhea called. I straightened my voice the way people do before answering recruiters.

“Hey,” she said.

“Hey.”

“You sound busy.”

"Yeah, chaos. Calls back-to-back." "Good chaos or bad chaos?" "Productive chaos," I lied.

There was a pause.

"You sure you're okay?" "Of course," I said, faking composure so hard it almost sounded real.

She sighed. "Lunch?"

"Half sandwich." You?"

"Coffee." "Still skipping meals and calling it hustle."

I smiled at the irony she couldn't see. You can't confess fear to someone already disappointed in you.

When the call ended, silence filled the room like unpaid rent.

Investor Syndrome

By afternoon, I was sweating through my only decent shirt. Zoom open. Investor smiling like a dentist.

"So, Aarav, the numbers?"

"Healthy pipeline. Conversion strong."

"Revenue?"

"Rising steadily."

"Clients?"

"Loyal."

Each lie stacked neatly, a house of cards built on caffeine and panic.

The call ended with his standard euthanasia:

"We'll revisit in December. Hang in there."

Investor language for we're out; good luck surviving winter.

I stared at my reflection in the black laptop screen, a salesman pitching confidence he didn't own.

For the first time in months, I felt the exhaustion of pretending to be someone still worth investing in.

When Even Messages Feel Heavy

Evening. Phone buzzed. Rhea calling.

I didn't pick up. Once, twice, three times.

I couldn't rehearse the performance again. The strength to sound "okay" had expired.

Her texts followed. Everything alright? Yeah. Just buried in work. You sure? Always.

Lie number eight. Smooth delivery. Zero return.

The chat window dimmed, but the word Always kept blinking, mocking me in the dark.

Pranav peeked in, half grin, half concern.

"She asked if you're fine?"

"Yeah."

"And you said yes?"

"Yeah." He nodded.

"Good. Keep rehearsing. One day you might even believe it."

He left.

The door clicked soft. Guilt stayed loud.

Crash Report

Later that night, I opened the app dashboard.

Users rising, revenue falling.
Like people , more engagement, less connection.
The irony wasn't lost on me: I'd built a product that measured communication while forgetting how to practice it.
The screen reflected my face, tired, pixelated, buffering.
I whispered, "What are you doing, Aarav?" No alert answered.
I almost called Rhea again, just to hear her voice, then stopped.
How do you tell someone you love that your dream might be dying, and it's your fault?

Meanwhile

Across the city, Simran looked up from her phone.
"Di, you're overthinking again."
Rhea didn't look away from the screen.
"He's pulling away."
"Maybe he's just tired."
"He's absent. That's different."
Simran sat beside her. "People vanish when they're drowning. It's not because they want distance, they just can't talk with water in their lungs."
Rhea's eyes softened. "That's poetic."
"It's true. Give him time to surface."
Rhea nodded, half comforted, half afraid she'd already waited too long.

Late-Night Honesty (With No One)

Past midnight. The city outside was quiet, that rare hour when even street dogs seemed introspective.
I typed an unsent note:

> Dear Rhea,
> I'm sorry I make optimism look like lying.
> The truth is,
> I'm scared. Not of failure, of you seeing me fail.
> I keep pretending I'm fine because the moment I admit I'm not, I'll have to start rebuilding everything, from code to confidence.
> You deserve a version of me that isn't buffering.

I didn't send it. Just saved it to drafts , my new folder for courage postponed.

Closing Beat

My laptop screen went black again, mirror and confession both. I looked at the faint reflection, a man still trying to reboot.
Maybe that's what failure really is, not the moment the world gives up on you, but when you start doing it first.
It wasn't failure yet. Just buffering.

Chapter 15

The Wrong Assumptions

Love misreads between the lines it never spoke.

The Fog Between Us

The week after that sleepless Thursday felt like walking through fog , everything visible, nothing clear. Rhea's messages grew shorter. Mine grew longer, emptier.

We were still "in touch." Technically. Our words had started social-distancing.

Same metro. Same time. She stood two poles away, scrolling like the screen owed her rescue. I wanted to say You look tired. But it sounded too much like I made you tired.

When the train braked, our shoulders brushed. Neither of us moved. Sometimes proximity only reminds you how far you've drifted.

Mixed Signals

Her texts came with timestamps now, not warmth:
Reached. Busy. Later.
Punctuation sharper than affection.
I told myself she was just stressed, overworked , maybe burnt out. I didn't say maybe burnt out on me.
At home, Pranav watched me over the TV glow.
"Still the happy couple?"
"We're fine."
"'Fine' is the ICU of relationships," he said.
Aditi called from the kitchen: "Try laughter; it's cheaper than therapy."
I tried. It didn't arrive.

The Missed Call

Thursday night. One ring. Her name flashed, then vanished.
I was mid-meeting, pitching optimism to a client who hadn't paid in three months. By the time I called back, her phone was unreachable.
Me: All okay? (no reply)
Three blinking dots, then nothing , like she'd typed forgiveness and deleted it.

Rhea's Side

Across the city, Rhea stared at her phone.

She had called on impulse, just wanted to hear Aarav's voice before her pitch. When he didn't pick up, pride spoke first.

Maybe he's busy. Maybe someone else is.

Either way, the need passed; embarrassment stayed.

Simran found her on the balcony, phone still in hand, eyes fixed on nothing. When Rhea didn't reach for the tea, Simran nudged the cup closer.

"You know," Simran said, "you two are geniuses at miscommunication."

Rhea glanced up, tired. "Meaning?"

"You keeps waiting for him to call, and he keeps waiting for you to read his silence. You two could automate heartbreak."

Rhea frowned. "Not funny."

"Neither is avoiding happiness," Simran said, the joke fading into honesty.

Rhea stared into the tea, the steam looked like something trying to rise but losing courage halfway.

"You and Aarav fought?"

"No. We're just... buffering."

"Ah, the modern breakup stage," Simran said lightly. "Stable Wi-Fi, unstable feelings."

Rhea chuckled despite herself. "You don't understand, Simran. It's not shouting or drama anymore, it's quiet. Too quiet."

"That's worse," Simran said softly. "Noise means hope; silence means the conclusion's already loading."

Rhea looked away. "You should write greeting cards for heartbreak."

"Already applied," Simran grinned. "They said I was too honest."

Rhea finally smiled, faint but real, the kind that hurts a little before it heals.

The Office Rumour

Friday. A colleague mentioned seeing me at a café, laughing with a female client. Rhea smiled politely, pretending her stomach hadn't twisted. Maybe it's work, she told herself. Maybe it's rebound research. That night, she didn't text. For the first time in months, her phone battery lasted till morning.

Aarav's Unravelling

I noticed the silence but blamed it on weather. Typed Long day? , deleted it. Scrolled old photos , the ones where she smiled like she trusted me.

Pranav leaned on my doorframe. "Call her." "Not tonight." Aditi's voice floated from the kitchen, gentle, firm: "You're mistaking ego for space."

She was right. But pride demanded one more night of self-importance.

The Morning After

Her message arrived next day: Good luck with your project today.

Short. Polite. Past tense of love.

I typed: Thanks. Miss you. Deleted Miss you. Sent Thanks.

At that same moment, my bank sent a notification: Account balance low. Poetic symmetry , finances and love life issuing identical warnings.

Crossing Lines

Evening rush hour. We landed in the same coach. She stood by the door; I pretended to check emails. Our reflections met first , two familiar strangers framed by motion.

I wanted to step closer. She stepped back.

The train braked hard at Rajiv Chowk. She got off without turning. I almost followed. Almost.

Rhea's Reflection

That night, she opened her planner. Wrote one line: We keep missing each other in the same city.

Underlined it twice. Closed the book.

If love is timing, ours had failed punctuation.

Aarav's Balcony

I sat on the balcony, same chair, same silence. A single diya from Diwali still sat unlit. Maybe endings don't come with darkness , maybe they come with refusal to shine.

"Maybe she's happier without me," I whispered. The air didn't disagree.

Some stories don't need villains , just two tired people and a few wrong assumptions.

The Father's Note

Later, Dad knocked softly and stepped out with two cups of tea. He set one down beside me. Didn't speak for a full minute.

Then, quietly: "Beta, people who love each other stop talking not because they stop caring, but because they start assuming the other already knows."

He looked at the sky. "Assumptions build silence faster than anger." He smiled faintly. "Call her before silence becomes habit."

He left the second cup behind. It went cold. But the warmth stayed.

Pranav's Text

At midnight, my phone buzzed.

Love fails when people start talking like lawyers and listening like witnesses. Pranav.

I didn't reply, but I saved it. Some advice ages better than apologies.

Closing Beat

The city slept. Only my screen still glowed. Her name on the chat , unread, unchanged, waiting.
We'd both built walls out of good intentions, convincing ourselves they were boundaries, not barriers.
And somewhere between those walls, our echoes started sounding like each other, familiar, but never close enough to touch.

Sometimes love doesn't end with anger.
Sometimes it just grows tired of explaining itself and slips into silence, believing that leaving quietly is the kindest way to stay remembered.

Chapter 16

Wedding Bells (Not Theirs)

Someone else's baraat, their own unfinished song.

The Summons

Beta, wedding season starts this weekend, Maa announced as if she were unveiling the Union Budget.

"Whose?" I asked, eyes still on my laptop.

"Your cousin Mehak's. Big event. Everyone's coming. You also."

"I have work."

Pranav looked up from his phone. "Work? You don't even have salary, forget schedule."

Aditi smirked. "He's coming. We need comic relief at family gatherings."

Maa added, "Rhea's family has also been invited."

That one landed like a bullet disguised as a ladoo. I looked up.

“What?”

Maa grinned. “Such a small world. Her father and Mehak’s father are colleagues. You two should patch up there.”

Before I could react, Aditi clapped her hands dramatically. “Perfect! Bollywood logic, Aarav, when love gives you a rerun, you don’t change the channel.”

Pranav leaned back, grinning. “Go, Romeo 2.0. Worst case, you get free dinner and closure.”

“Both of you are insane,” I said.

Aditi leaned closer, tone softening beneath her grin. “Listen, idiot. When something real finds you, don’t let ego play referee. Life doesn’t hand out sequels easily.”

I tried to laugh it off, but her words stayed, too filmy to dismiss, too true to ignore.

Pranav raised an imaginary toast. “ **Operation Patch-Up**, to love and weddings, may both get their happy endings tonight.”

Maa looked pleased, destiny already finalised.

And just like that, my weekend changed shape. The mission had a venue, a deadline, and one impossible objective: “*make Rhea smile again before the night ended.*”

At Rhea's home.

Simran adjusted Rhea's saree.

"Saree, gold earrings, diplomatic smile, perfect armour."

"It's not war," Rhea said.

"Then why do you look like you're marching to one?"

Rhea laughed. "Because peace treaties with ex-almosts are tricky."

Simran winked. "Then win the after-party, not the argument."

The Hall of Noise

The banquet hall looked like someone threw a Pinterest board at a chandelier.

People shimmered, music thumped, and one uncle was already taking selfies like they were tax-deductible.

Pranav led the way, shaking hands with relatives he didn't remember.

Aditi whispered, "Smile, eat, and whatever you do, don't start your philosophy near the buffet."

I nodded , too distracted. She followed my gaze and smirked. "Found her?"

There she was , across the hall. Gold saree. Hair open. Laugh small but real. She looked like peace dressed for the occasion.

The Unavoidable Collision

We saw each other the way accidents happen , slow, visible, unstoppable.

Her eyes met mine, then moved past politely, like checking weather she already knew. I moved closer anyway.

"Hi."

"Hi."

Her smile was gentle, like an HR email acknowledging your resignation.

"You look..."

"Please don't," she said softly, saving me from adjectives.

The DJ switched from Tum Hi Ho to Desi Girl. Cosmic joke.

"How's work?" she asked.

"Surviving. Still in stealth mode."

"You?"

"New campaign. Big client."

We both nodded , the international sign for we're not ready to talk about us.

Relatives, Drama & Collateral Damage

Enter Chachi, a human firecracker wrapped in silk.

"Aarav beta! Stand straight! Rhea beti, you here too! Dekho, colour coordination! Destiny!"

Rhea smiled, trapped politeness. "Aunty, pure coincidence."

"Coincidences are God's to-do list," Chachi declared, calling over the photographer.
Pranav appeared, phone raised. "Family picture , for evidence!"

Aditi pulled it down. "Stop it. You're violating privacy policies."
Pranav: "Comfortable people don't make good stories."
Rhea's mother joined in, warmth personified.
"Aarav beta, good to see you. Hope you're doing well."
"Yes, Aunty. Still figuring adulthood."
"Do it quickly," she smiled. "Marriage follows soon."
Pranav: "Direct hit."
Aditi: "Collateral laughter."
I wanted to disappear into the dessert counter.

The Buffet Line Philosophy

In the paneer tikka queue, Rhea ended up behind me.
We reached for the same plate.
"Go ahead," I said.
"Thanks."
We served in silence , awkward, synchronized, tragicomic.
"You look tired," she said finally.
"So do you."

"Long weeks."

"Long silences too," I muttered.

Her eyes lifted , steady, sharp. "I didn't know if you wanted to talk."

"I always did. Didn't know if you'd listen."

"I was listening," she said softly. "You just weren't saying anything real."

The sizzler tray hissed, punctuation for two people burning politely.

The Courtyard Escape

We slipped out to the quieter courtyard, the air cooler, lights trembling on the fountain. Inside, laughter echoed like reminders from another life.

"So how's the start-up?" she asked, arms crossed.

"Still standing. Lean, broke, caffeinated. Lost one investor, gained anxiety."

"Progress?" she smiled faintly.

I grinned. "You?"

"Running a campaign that won't sleep. But I'm good tired. Not broken tired."

We stood a moment longer than courtesy allowed.

She said, "You know, being honest about fear looks better on you than fake confidence."

"Honesty's cheaper," I said. "No PR budget required."

For the first time in weeks, the air between us didn't sting.

Pranav shouted from inside, "Aarav! Baraat's here! Go dance before the groom changes his mind!"
Rhea laughed, real, spontaneous, beautiful. That sound did something to my ribs.

The Corridor Moment

As the crowd poured out to greet the groom, we drifted near a side corridor, music muffled, perfume heavy.
"I missed this," I said.
"Weddings?"
"No. You-smiling."
"Don't start," she warned. "I'm on my best etiquette setting."
"I'm not starting. Just remembering."
"Remembering isn't enough, Aarav. That's nostalgia with better lighting."
"I know. I'm trying to write new chapters."
She hesitated, softened. "Maybe just start with punctuation. End sentences before they become walls."
Someone called her name from inside. I wanted to say drive safe, but that felt too small for the lump in my throat.
She turned to go, then glanced back. "Try to dance. You look less sad in motion."
"Only if you promise to watch."

"I might," she said, walking away, half promise, half peace treaty.

The Baraat Chaos

Drums rolled. Uncles in sequins went to war with rhythm. I stood near the gate, pretending to clap while scanning for her face.

Aditi joined me, holding a gulab jamun. "So, reconciliation status?"

"Pending," I said.

"Communication protocol rebooting." "Then dance," she said, shoving the sweet at me. "Hope burns calories."

Pranav appeared, sweaty and ecstatic. "You danced?"

"I moved rhythm-adjacent." (I danced badly, but with heart.) "That counts. Proud of you."

He grinned, "You know, you two are the best family drama since Yeh Jawaani Hai Deewani."

"Only difference," I said, "ours is running without an editor."

Closing Beat

The drums rolled outside, relatives screamed "Badhai ho!", and sparklers fought the night air.

I stood by the gate, scanning the courtyard where she'd been a little while ago, only fairy lights now, no trace of her laughter. Every word I hadn't said pressed against my throat.

That's when my cousin appeared beside me, mouth full of dessert. "Rhea left early," he said casually. "Her college friend's wedding, same hotel, next lawn."

Pranav looked up from his phone. "Another wedding? Delhi's version of parallel universes."

Aditi nudged him. "You know what that means." He grinned. "Sequel."

Aditi turned to me, her tone suddenly soft. "When love knocks twice, Aarav, don't check caller ID."

Maybe the universe wasn't offering second chances, it was daring me to earn one. I smiled faintly. Too late for caller ID. This was a rescue mission now.

The night split into two weddings and one unfinished story. Somewhere between the drums and the silence, I decided, tonight I find her, and I don't leave till I do.

Outside, the drums softened into distance; the hall lights bled into the night like tired fireworks. I glanced toward the corridor connecting both lawns, the air still thick with perfume, noise, and unfinished sentences.

Maybe love wasn't lost; it had just changed venues. And before doubt could argue, my feet were already walking.

Chapter 17

The Gatecrash

What could go wrong when regret crashes a wedding?

Wrong Address, Right Mistake

Rhea had left early, her friend's wedding, next lawn, same hotel. The corridor connecting both halls smelled of perfume, diesel, and decisions.

I could still hear my mother laughing somewhere behind me, Pranav yelling "hero mode activated," and Aditi calling out, "Try not to trend on Instagram this time."

Too late. My shoes were already echoing toward the second gate.

I walked toward the corridor connecting the two lawns , same compound, two worlds apart. One for family; one for unfinished business.

Mission: reconciliation.

Deadline: tonight.

The adjoining lawn blazed like a festival , fairy lights tangled in ambition, music loud enough to rearrange regrets.

I took a breath and walked in as if I belonged, which technically I didn't.

At Delhi weddings, confidence is the dress code. For the first ten seconds, it worked.

Then I saw her, or so I thought. Gold saree, same hair, same tilt of the head. "Rhea!" I called, half-hope, half-hallucination. She turned.

Not Rhea. Definitely different lady, now scandalised and clutching a plate of halwa.

An uncle blinked. "Beta, groom's side?"
"Emotionally, yes," I said.

Laughter rippled. Someone pulled my hand; someone else shouted, "Dance, bhai!"

And just like that, the universe pressed play on another mistake.

Mission Improbable

Within seconds, I was in the centre of the storm , a baraat remix spinning out of control, cousins cheering like investors in bad stock, and me, performing what could only be described as interpretive cardio.

The DJ screamed, "Mauka hai mauka!" I screamed internally.

A kid splashed rose water across my face; an aunty, possessed by hospitality, stuffed a laddoo into my mouth mid-spin; an uncle tried to twirl me, both of us nearly achieved enlightenment.

The photographer barked, "Smile!" I did. Tragedy always looks better lit.

Then someone shouted, "Gatecrasher!" I raised both hands. "Guest... from the parallel universe." They laughed. Because Delhi weddings forgive everything , except low energy.

At some point, I found myself leading a conga line of strangers who believed enthusiasm was choreography. Aunty cheered, "So filmy!"

Feeling inspired, I tried a twirl, forgetting ten people were attached behind me, and almost caused a mass emotional collision.

Somewhere between Gallan Goodiyan and oxygen deprivation, it hit me, Rhea wasn't here.

Wrong crowd. Right emotion.

The DJ yelled "Once more!"; my lungs filed a complaint.

I used the next beat drop as my exit cue and slipped out through a hedge, confetti in my hair, halwa on my sleeve, and regret doing push-ups inside my chest.

Collision Course

I slipped back through the hedge, back toward the first wedding's corridor, same lights, same noise, only my dignity missing in action.

The air between the two lawns buzzed with leftover music, the kind that refuses to end even when the song does.

And there she was, Rhea, standing right at the crossroads where both worlds met.

Half-lit by the fairy lights from her friend's wedding, half-shadowed by mine. Aditi was beside her, holding a phone, probably live-texting Pranav with "he actually showed up."

Rhea's expression said she already knew about my uninvited performance. Arms folded. Eyes sharp. That smile, just waiting to turn into either forgiveness or murder.

"Quite an entrance," she said.

"Accidental," I replied. "Turns out Google Maps doesn't cover emotional stupidity."

Aditi, sensing danger, quietly stepped back, then vanished into the crowd like a trained spy.

Rhea tilted her head. "So, you gatecrashed another wedding?"

"Technically, I was following love. The gate just happened to be in the way."

She exhaled, half amused, half furious. "You think chaos is romantic?"

"No," I said quietly. "But silence was killing me. I needed motion, even if it was in the wrong direction."

Her glare softened just enough for the moonlight to slip through.

"You're impossible."

"I'm consistent."

"Consistently stupid."

"Progress. Last month, I was spineless."

That made her laugh, unwillingly, but it escaped anyway. The kind of laugh that sounds like the night forgiving you for existing.

She shook her head, trying to hide the smile. "Go back, Aarav. This isn't your scene."

"Maybe not," I said, "but you still are."

The Universe Adds Props

And just when the silence between us was starting to sound like a decision, the universe, ever dramatic, sent in backup.

From the driveway rolled the flower vendor, same wiry frame, same bicycle stacked with marigolds like portable sunshine.

Rhea laughed at the vendor. "You again?"

He grinned wider. "Madam remembers! Same jodi, same flowers!"

"Persistent, aren't you?" I said, glancing at him, half amused, half resigned.

The vendor winked. "Fate gives EMI, sir, pay in instalments."

Before I could protest, he tossed a garland over my neck, a floral drive-by blessing, and pedalled off, leaving petals, perfume, and prophecy hanging in the air.

Rhea's laugh burst out before she could stop it, bright, ridiculous, human. That laugh hit harder than any apology ever could.

For a second, everything around us paused, two weddings, one night, and the faint smell of marigolds deciding whose story they'd decorate.

Then someone from her side called her name. She turned, still smiling, and walked toward the second lawn, where music and destiny were both waiting for the encore.

I watched her disappear into the second lawn.

Truth in Surround Sound

The laughter faded, but its echo stayed, like background music that didn't want to end.

I could still see her half-smile in my head, the one she wore when she didn't fully trust the moment yet.

I took a step forward anyway, as if the air she'd left behind could still hear me.

"I messed up," I said quietly, to no one and everyone. "I hid behind work, behind pride. I made silence look like maturity. It wasn't. It was fear wearing a tie."

Her absence listened better than her presence ever could.

The DJ, oblivious to personal turning points, switched to a slow track. Lights softened until they felt like confession lamps.

Rhea's laughter from earlier replayed in my mind, half disbelief, half forgiveness, until the fireworks outside added their unnecessary percussion.

Petals from the garland clung to my jacket like proof that the universe had a sense of humour. I leaned against the railing, catching my breath, listening to two weddings playing two different songs, one beat for chaos, one for calm.

Maybe love sounded exactly like this: two rhythms overlapping, refusing to sync, yet somehow making sense together.

The Emotional Punchline

I stood for a moment, staring at the corridor that now smelled of rain and rosewater. A minute ago, it had been a battlefield; now, it felt like a checkpoint.

I laughed under my breath. "Some people get closure. I get choreography and garlands."

Pranav appeared with his plate of snacks. "Update?"

"Half victory," I said. "The target laughed. Then escaped."

Aditi joined, eyes still amused. "That laugh sounded dangerously close to forgiveness."

"Or pity," I said.

She shrugged. "Take whichever leads to coffee."

The drums from Rhea's friend's wedding rolled again. Somebody tested the mic; the sharp feedback tore through the night. I looked toward the second lawn where lights pulsed like a heartbeat trying to find rhythm.

Maybe this wasn't failure. Maybe this was intermission. And if the universe wanted an encore, I wasn't about to leave before the song ended.

Pranav's Review

Pranav raised an imaginary toast. "**To Operation Patch-Up**," he said, "may the groom dance and the almost-exes finally talk."

Aditi laughed. "Let's just hope they finally talk before the night ends."

I smiled, tightening the garland still hanging around my neck. "Round two," I said. "Wish me luck."

Pranav grinned. "Luck? You need lighting."

Closing Beat

I turned toward the second lawn, Rhea's friend's wedding, music louder now, laughter brighter, the universe clearly not done with us yet.

Fireworks flared once more across the courtyard, petals floated through the air like applause from unseen hands. I walked forward, heart hammering in time with the dhol.

Maybe love doesn't arrive on time. Maybe it gatecrashes, messes up the choreography, and still demands one last song.

Chapter 18

Microphone Mishap

The loudest love confession ever accidentally delivered.

The Sound of Chance

The fireworks had quieted, but the music hadn't. From the next lawn, Rhea's friend's wedding was still alive , laughter, lights, and the same DJ who believed volume healed heartbreak.

I crossed the courtyard, still wearing the marigold garland the universe had forced on me. Every step felt equal parts fear and stubbornness.

Inside, the crowd recognised me instantly.

"Arre, the dancer's back!" someone shouted.

Another yelled, "Come save the stage again!"

Laughter followed , friendly now, not mocking.

Rhea was near the stage, talking to her friends, pretending not to notice me.

That was progress. Earlier, she'd have left.

I found a quiet corner and tried to gather courage.

All I needed was a minute to say what I hadn't said in months.

But Delhi weddings don't give you minutes, they give you microphones.

The Call of the Mic

The DJ spotted me mid-thought.

"Ladies and gentlemen," he boomed, "our dancing hero is back! "Give him the mic for a few words before we cut the cake!"

Before I could vanish behind the food counter, someone shoved a microphone into my hand.

The crowd cheered. The same people who'd seen me nearly collapse were now expecting a speech.

Rhea froze mid-conversation.

My soul filed for resignation.

I cleared my throat. "Uh... good evening."

The mic whined, the crowd chuckled, my voice cracked like adolescence revisited.

"Not exactly from the groom's side," I said. "More from the damage-control department of my own life."

A ripple of laughter.

Even Rhea smiled , the reluctant kind that says please stop, *but also, don't.*

The Hijack

I don't know what possessed me, maybe the leftover adrenaline, maybe guilt, maybe Delhi itself, but truth slipped out before dignity could stop it.

"I came here because someone I care about is here," I said. "She doesn't know what I'm going to speak, and she definitely doesn't know how much silence I've mistaken for maturity."

The crowd quieted. Even the waiters froze mid-pour.

I took a deep breath. "Start-ups teach you to pitch till someone believes you. Tonight, I'm pitching... feelings. No investors. Just witnesses."

The DJ whispered, "Wah bhai, heartbreak with PowerPoint energy."

Laughter again, this time softer, understanding.

Rhea tried to hide her smile. Small victory. I took it.

The Heart on Loudspeaker

"I'm sorry," I said, voice steadier now.

"For calling distance independence."

"For calling ego self-respect."

For thinking "love needed strategy instead of courage."

A hush spread like oxygen returning to a room.

"I thought silence was noble. Turns out it's just fear with better vocabulary."

I looked at her directly. "I love her. Not in the movie way, in the chai-at-5 p.m. way."

"The kind that survives bad Wi-Fi and worse moods. The kind that still shows up after the wrong wedding."

Applause broke out, hesitant, then wholehearted.

Rhea's expression softened: disbelief, pride, and something dangerously close to forgiveness.

The Mishap

And right when the moment turned sacred, the DJ's assistant yelled, "Bhai-saab, cake-cutting time!" Music exploded , Gallan Goodiyan!

My mic was still on. Everyone heard me mutter, "Cake-cutting ho ya heart-cutting, main toh gaya."

The hall erupted.

Laughter, whistles, applause.

Even Rhea doubled over, laughing through tears. The groom high-fived me. I'd just upstaged his wedding, again.

And for once, my blunder didn't feel like disaster. It felt like grace disguised as comedy.

After the Noise

When the crowd finally dispersed, I found her outside near the fountain. Rain had started, light, uncertain, like the city was blushing.

She stood there, hair damp, expression half-amused, half-exasperated.

"That was insane," she said.

"I was improvising."

"You turned my friend's wedding into a TED Talk."

"I paid emotional rent. The venue came free."

"You didn't have to say all that in public."

"I did. Private apologies never reached you. This one had better acoustics."

She shook her head, smiling despite herself. "You're unbelievable."

"I'm consistent."

"Consistently dramatic."

"Progress. Last month, I was spineless."

That made her laugh, the real one.

The kind that sounds like forgiveness tuning its frequency.

The Honest Ending

"I don't know where we go from here," I said quietly. "But I know I'm done editing honesty."

She looked at me for a long moment. Rain caught in her hair like punctuation marks.

"You didn't trust me with the messy parts," she said softly. "Next time, try mess before silence."

I nodded. "Version 2.0. Fewer bugs, better bandwidth."

She tried to smile, but a tear escaped, quiet, unannounced.
It wasn't sorrow. It was relief wearing the wrong costume.
Her hand brushed mine, brief, deliberate, enough to rewrite everything unsaid.
"Tomorrow," she whispered. "Coffee. No mic."
"Promise."
She blinked away what the rain had already claimed.

"Finally," she said, smiling through it, "you learned to speak before the moment ends."

Closing Beat

Thunder rolled somewhere above, as if the sky itself clapped a second too late.
Inside, the DJ switched to *Tera Ban Jaunga,* love on replay for a city that never apologises for being loud.
Rhea turned once before stepping back inside, wet hair, half-smile, courage in her eyes.
It wasn't a *yes*.
It was something rarer, a restart.
The city roared beyond laughter, beats, horns, and rain merging into applause no one orchestrated.
I stood by the fountain, drenched, smiling like a fool who'd finally stopped hiding.

Love doesn't wait for perfection.
It just waits for you to speak before silence writes the ending.
Rain didn't fall harder; it just stayed longer, soft, forgiving, almost musical.
And by the time the last dhol faded, the lawns were quiet again.
Some storms don't break.
They just teach you how to stand still

Chapter 19

Truths Unveiled

When the music stops, honesty finally finds its turn at the mic.

The Morning After

Delhi looked washed in leftover light, grey sky, still air, and the faint smell of last night's fireworks dissolving into morning traffic.

I walked out of my room late, hair still a mess, heart still inconveniently hopeful. Pranav looked up from his laptop. "Alive?"

"Barely," I said.

Aditi didn't look up. "We saw the video."

"What video?" She turned her screen. There I was, marigolds, mic, and mild insanity, trending with the caption 'When Start-up Guy Confesses Mid-Wedding.'

I groaned. "Perfect. Now my love life has analytics."

Pranav grinned. "Relax, at least this pitch got applause."

For the first time in weeks, I didn't mind being the joke. Maybe because it finally belonged to me.

The Message

Around noon, my phone buzzed. One unread message.

Rhea: Coffee. 6 p.m., no microphones allowed.

I smiled. The universe was mercifully learning brevity.

Owning Up

"I don't know where to start," I said.

"Start where you stopped pretending," she answered.

I inhaled. "The start-up's struggling. Has been for months. I kept lying because I didn't want you to see me failing. I thought if I looked steady, maybe you'd stay."

She listened, no judgment, just quiet focus. "So you built a wall," she said. "And called it protection."

"Yeah. Turns out walls block oxygen too."

Her mouth softened. "You don't need to impress me, Aarav. You just need to let me in before the damage-control meeting."

I laughed, small, grateful. "I'm learning."

"You're late," she said , gentle, not cruel.

Her Side of Truth

"My late-night calls?" she continued. "They were investor calls. I'm launching my own design studio."

I blinked. "So Karan wasn't..."

She smirked. "My boss. Not my plot twist."

Relief cracked a laugh out of me. "You realise I've hated a man for nothing?"

"Welcome to gender equality," she said. "We all suffer assumptions."

We both laughed, first shared laugh in weeks. It landed softly, like rain on dust.

Under the Surface

"You know what hurt?" she said. "Not the doubt. The distance. You kept showing the edited version of yourself."

"I thought honesty would scare you."

"It would've," she said. "But lies bored me more."

The honesty between us thickened, awkward, fragile, healing. I reached across the table; her fingers hesitated, then stayed.

Warmth. Not forgiveness yet, but the road to it.

The Core Truth

"I used to think love was about getting everything right," I said.

"She showed me it's about being wrong, and still being held together."

Rhea's eyes softened. "Then stop performing. Build slow." "Like a beta version?" She smiled. "Exactly. Love v2.0 , with patch notes and less ego."

The Departure Scene

Evening spilled gold through the window. The waiter left the bill as though afraid to break something sacred. Outside, Delhi honked itself back to reality.

Rhea stood. "We're okay?" "We're real,"

I said. "Real is good."

At the door, she turned. "You didn't need a microphone to tell me you loved me."

"I did," I smiled. "Otherwise, I'd have whispered it into another silence."

She laughed, soft, forgiving, almost home. "Next time," she said, "speak before the mic finds you."

Closing Beat

She walked away, her hair catching the evening light. For the first time, the city didn't look like chaos, it looked like a pause between songs.

That day, love didn't need applause. It just needed two people choosing honesty over history.

Not a reunion, just two voices finally tuned to the same frequency of truth. Some truths don't arrive to applause. They arrive quietly.

Chapter 20

The Grand Gesture

PowerPoint, samosas, and the courage to reboot love.

The Idea That Wouldn't Sleep

Rhea's words kept looping in my head: "**You didn't trust me with the messy parts.**"

That line didn't sting , it haunted, like an unpaid electricity bill flashing red in my subconscious.

So, I decided to do the one thing I'd avoided all along: show her everything messy. Not roses, not violins , something painfully, hilariously real.

Pranav called it Project Redemption - The Finale.

Aditi sighed. "Just don't propose with PowerPoint this time."

The Setup

Saturday morning, I called her. “Can you drop by around six, to my workspace?”

“Your bedroom doesn’t count as office space.”

“It does now , temporary headquarters. No dress code, snacks provided.”

She exhaled. “Fine. But if I see a microphone, I’m leaving.”

“No mic. Pinky promise.”

I cleaned like a man on a redemption deadline. Fairy lights, coffee cups, one cleared table. By the end, my “workspace” looked like an emotional audit report, half effort, half faith.

The Leak

Pranav peeked in, munching chips. “Maa’s asking why you’re vacuuming. Should I tell her investor visit or proposal attempt?”

“Investor,” I said too fast.

He grinned. “Good. Because she already called Rhea’s mother to ‘bless the partnership.’”

“What?!” “Your blue tick betrayed you.

Never underestimate Indian mothers and last-seen timestamps.”

Aditi entered, whispering, “Congrats. Your surprise now has public shareholders.”

I buried my face in a cushion. “Universe, take me private again.”

The Arrival

At six, the bell rang. Rhea entered , calm, elegant, wary. The kind of entrance that makes air behave.

"What is this?" she asked.

"My confession, part two," I said.

"Quarterly review edition." She folded her arms. "You actually made slides?"

"PowerPoint heals faster than poetry."

On the wall: Quarterly Review: Us.

She laughed despite herself.

"You're unbelievable."

"Consistent," I said. "Please take your seat. There will be snacks."

The Presentation

Slide 1 - Q1 Highlights

A photo from our first coffee, the "wrong swipe" that spilled more cappuccino than confidence. I grinned. "You called it premium service."

She laughed. "And you corrected the barista, Aarav with two A's."

"Brand consistency," I said.

Her smile softened. "And chaos with charm." That was our first quarter, spilled coffee, over-explaining vowels, and something neither of us had planned but couldn't log out of.

Slide 2 - Q2 Challenges

Two mugs on a desk, one chipped.

"The project from hell," I said.

Rhea smiled. "You mean teamwork with extra caffeine."

"The projector died, but we didn't."

"You handled code; I handled crisis."

"Communication gap," I admitted.

"You mean your emotional Wi-Fi was down," she teased.

That quarter taught us debugging isn't just for software, it's for people too.

Slide 3 - Q3 Crisis Management

A still of the wedding stage, captioned *Man confesses via DJ mic.*

She burst out laughing. "That's your portfolio image?"

"Engagement metrics were excellent."

Slide 4 - Q4 Future Forecast

Just one line: **No More Hiding.**

Silence.

The last slide faded to white.

For a moment, neither of us spoke. Even the fan seemed to wait for data input.

I closed the laptop slowly. "That's the pitch," I said. "Four quarters, a lot of bugs, one working connection."

Rhea stayed quiet, gaze still on the screen.

"I don't know where this story goes next," I said softly. "I don't know if my start-up survives next year, or if I do. But I know I want you in every plan , even the failing ones. No scripts, no filters. Just bandwidth, honesty, and enough coffee to survive us."

Her expression changed , no tears, no drama, just that slow, thawing warmth I'd missed for months.

Then she smiled, small and sure.

"Typical," she said. "Even your love confessions need slides."

"Consistent," I replied. "Quarterly reviews build accountability."

She shook her head, smiling wider. "You're impossible."

"Statistically true," I said.

And for the first time, the silence between us didn't feel like waiting. It felt like arrival.

The Power Cut

The screen went black.

So did the room.

For a heartbeat, there was only the hum of the city outside and our uneven breathing.

Then, one by one, the fairy lights blinked back to life, hesitant, like they were testing hope.

"Typical," she said softly. "Even electricity's emotional around you."

I smiled in the half-light. "Maybe it just wants an answer."

She took a slow step closer, the glow catching her in pieces, eyes, smile, disbelief, something dangerously close to yes.

"That's a yes," she whispered finally.

And the lights, as if relieved, stayed steady.

The Family Interruption

Right then, Maa entered with divine comic timing.

"Aarav beta, oh! Rhea!" She gasped, hand on heart. "Perfect!"

"Maa!"

Rhea's laughter collapsed into helpless bursts.

Pranav leaned in from the hallway. "We told her it's an engagement dry run."

Rhea wiped her eyes. "Your family needs a web series."

Aditi added, "Season 1 ends today."

The Aftermath

When calm returned, Rhea shook her head, still smiling. "You're impossible."

"I'm consistent."

"But you've changed."

"I had to. Turns out vulnerability scales better than arrogance."

"You're really pitching love like a business model?"

"Beta version: fewer bugs, better uptime."

She stepped closer. "Then consider me your beta tester."

That did it. I laughed , the first laugh that didn't hide fear.

The Gesture

I handed her a small keychain, silver, simple, engraved: *Co-Founder, Life Inc.*

"Too much?" I asked, half-joking, half-hoping she'd get what I meant.

She turned it over in her palm, smiling. "Perfectly on brand," she said.

Of course she did, Rhea always understood my language: half jokes, half honesty, all heart hidden in humour.

"Let's build something, Aarav. No investors, no exit plan."

"Agreed," I said. "But the unlimited-snacks clause stays."

She laughed, then smiled, the kind of smile that ends wars quietly.

Closing Beat

Later, we sat cross-legged on the floor, cold samosas between us, city lights blinking through the balcony glass.

Her head rested on my shoulder; my heartbeat finally matched the ceiling fan's rhythm.

"So," she murmured, "what's next?"

"Maintenance phase," I said. "Quarterly reviews. Infinite coffee."

"And honesty."

"Non-negotiable."

She smiled into my shirt. "Good."

Outside, the streetlights shimmered like tiny affirmations. Inside, everything felt small, steady, and enough.

Some grand gestures aren't loud.

They're just two people rebuilding the same room they once left broken, choosing to stay until the lights come back on.

Not fireworks.

Just light, finally steady, finally shared.

Chapter 21

Holi of Love

Colours mend what words once broke.

Morning Colours

If Diwali burned bridges, Holi washed the ash. The colony courtyard bloomed like an overexcited rainbow , buckets of colour, pichkaris armed, uncles discovering arthritis mid-dance, aunties wielding plates of gujiya like ammunition. Kids shrieked through clouds of pink. The dhol thumped in happy defiance of rhythm.

I stood with a bucket, pretending calm.

Pranav eyed the crowd. “Target or truce?”

“Truce until betrayal.”

Aditi grinned. “You two won’t last more than three minutes before chaos starts.”

Our truce felt like our love, fragile, hilarious, one splash away from turning real. Beneath the noise, hope pulsed quietly. I knew she'd come.

The Entrance

When Rhea stepped through the gate, the courtyard forgot to breathe.

White kurta. Hair half tied, half free. A faint line of pink already brushed across her cheek, an early warning of beauty in motion. The sunlight bent slightly to accommodate her.

She spotted me, and that look, equal parts mischief and memory, a half-smile that said: *Don't start unless you can finish.*

It was enough to turn Delhi's chaos into background music.

"You came," I said.

"Your mother sent three reminders and one threat."

"Her conversion rate is remarkable."

Rhea smiled. "She should run your investor meetings."

The air between us shimmered, the kind of silence that hums, not hides.

The First Splash

Chachi materialised like fate with a thali of colour.

"Aarav beta, Rhea beti, together-together, auspicious start!"

Before we could react, she smeared bright pink across both our faces. “See? Perfect match!”

Pranav: “Breaking news: merger announced on festival day!”

Aditi threw colour at him. “Behave, shareholder of chaos!”

From across the courtyard, Simran yelled, “Save some colour for real weddings!”

Rhea threw a handful of pink dust in her direction. “Manifesting, not announcing!”

Simran ducked. “Fine line, sister!”

I grinned. “Your sister’s worse than my brother.”

“Genetic gift,” Rhea said.

Rhea laughed, that laugh. Bright. Effortless. The kind that makes your heart forget it was ever bruised.

The Colour and the Pause

We drifted toward the quieter edge of the courtyard, near the old fountain. Music thumped somewhere behind us; here, time just... slowed.

“No microphones today?” she teased, dipping her fingers into red.

“None,” I said.

“Good. I prefer organic confession mediums.”

She lifted her hand, brushed a streak of colour across my cheek, slow, deliberate, reverent. It wasn’t play; it was declaration.

The world around us blurred into laughter and water fights, but in our tiny corner, colour and heartbeat synced.

I dipped my fingers into blue and touched her forehead gently. She closed her eyes, trusting, serene, and whispered, "This feels different."

"It is," I said. "No fear left to hide behind."

The red and blue blended on her skin, turning violet, the shade of something reborn.

The Breath Between

Then the first raindrop fell.

Someone gasped. Then laughter. Then rain, a hundred silver threads stitching chaos into unity.

She looked up, water tracing her face.

"You're staring," she said.

"I'm memorising," I answered.

Our palms met, wet colour bleeding into new shades.

"I used to think love was noise," I said.

"And now?" she asked.

"Now it's this, the silence before it becomes a promise."

Rhea smiled, soft as surrender.

Then she dipped her fingers in red and covered my eyes.

"Now," she whispered, "even if the world looks, they'll only see us."

I laughed, blind, free.

When she lifted her hand, her thumb traced my jaw, steady, sure.

And then she kissed me.

Not fireworks. Warmth.

Not a performance. Peace.

A kiss that steadied the storm instead of starting one, an exchange of apology and oxygen.

She whispered against my lips, “This is my favourite version of you, the one that doesn’t hide.”

“Then I’ll stay visible,” I said.

Rain fell harder. Colour ran softer. The world blurred into a painting of second chances.

The World Intrudes

“Finally!” Pranav’s voice, gleeful as thunder. “Public beta testing complete!”

Aditi added, “Get a room, or at least an umbrella!”

We turned, laughing and blushing and utterly unbothered.

Flower-vendor uncle appeared, marigolds around his neck, drunk on thandai and happiness.

“Blessed union!” he shouted, scattering petals like blessings coded in chaos.

Chachi clasped her hands dramatically. “Rang lag gaya, shaadi pakki!”

Even the dhol player nodded like a man who’d seen divine timing.

We gave up trying to look dignified. Instead, we danced, rain-soaked, ridiculous, radiant. And for once, Delhi felt exactly like home.

After the Rain

As the downpour eased, colour settled into calm pastels.

Rhea looked at me, drenched, glowing. "We could've fixed all this months ago if we'd just talked."

"True," I said, brushing a strand of hair from her face. "But then we'd have missed this scene."

She laughed, warm and exasperated. "You're impossible."

"Consistent."

We stood there, fingers interlaced, watching the last streaks of colour sink into earth, and I realised love wasn't a second chance. It was the first real one.

Closing Beat

Around us, people packed up, umbrellas bloomed, music faded. We stayed, drenched, smiling, still slightly shivering, but refusing to move.

The fountain gurgled beside us; rain dripped from the wires above like applause in Morse code.

Rhea leaned into my shoulder. "So... this is us now?"

"This is us," I said.

"No hashtags?"

"Only one."

"What?"

"#Finally."

She laughed, and in that sound, the city, the chaos, the heartbreak, everything softened into colour we could finally keep.

Some stories don't end with closure. They end with rain that knows where to fall.

Not the end, just colour settling into love that finally learned to stay.

Chapter 22

Swiping Forward

Some wrong swipes are just right, eventually.

New Beginnings

A few months after Holi, life rearranged itself quietly. The world around us didn't change, we did.

Families stopped asking "What next?" and started saying "Take care." Our engagement was small , close family, too much food, just enough laughter. No fireworks, no chaos. Only that soft, trembling peace that comes when you finally stop running and start arriving.

Then came the offer that changed everything, an investor at Gurugram, who believed not just in our start-up, but in the way Rhea and I finished each other's half-sentences.

It wasn't just funding; it was faith. Maybe love and ambition could finally share the same Wi-Fi connection.

So we moved to Gurugram, two rooms, one balcony, one overworked coffee machine. Everyone called it practical. We called it home.

That first night, we sat among unopened boxes, eating noodles from paper cups.

Rhea leaned on my shoulder. "Feels strange, doesn't it?"

"Not strange," I said. "Just right."

The City of Beginnings

Gurugram sounded like ambition, glass towers, glowing logos, chai stalls that stayed open past midnight. We built our days around code, coffee, and the comfort of each other's chaos.

Sometimes she worked till 2 a.m., hair falling across the keyboard. I'd quietly slide a cup of coffee near her elbow, and she'd smile without looking up, a smile that said I know you're there. A small acknowledgment that love doesn't need ceremony.

Our balcony faced the skyline. At night, we'd watch planes blink through the haze. Each one felt like a promise, a reminder that it's okay to take off again after turbulence.

Everyday Love

Morning chaos: two toothbrushes arguing for sink space. Her playlists louder than my patience. My T-shirts migrating mysteriously to her side of the cupboard. Breakfasts half-burnt but always shared.

Love, it turned out, wasn't the grand gestures, it was the rhythm between small ones.

The way she said, "Don't forget to breathe," when I lost track of days. The way I said, "Take a break," when her eyes dimmed behind deadlines. She kept my timelines; I kept her calm. That's how the ledger stayed balanced.

Quiet Evenings

Work slowed with sunset. I'd find her by the balcony rail, watching the city glow, the skyline like circuitry lit by collective hope.

I'd wrap my arms around her, chin resting on her shoulder. "Still scared?" she'd ask.

"Of what?"

"Of losing this."

I tightened my hold. "Not anymore."

It wasn't a promise, just a quiet truth. Peace, it turns out, is louder than passion when you've fought for it together.

The Swiping-Forward Moment

One humid night, her phone buzzed, a relic of an old app flashing a ghost notification: "Find your match this monsoon!"

Rhea laughed. "Persistent, aren't they?" "Tell them my search ended seasons ago," I said.

She smiled. "Then keep the window open. We're still growing."

She curled into my lap, forehead resting against mine. "Remember the first swipe?"

"How could I forget? You almost unmatched."

"I almost did," she said softly. "Good thing hope had faster reflexes."

(Translation : "I almost gave up, but something, hope, instinct, love, reacted before I could.")

The smell of rain drifted in, familiar, forgiving. Like the same night that started it all, only softer now, calmer, surer.

We still fought about groceries and deadlines. We still made up over coffee and bad jokes. But now, even our silences felt safe, not walls, just pauses.

Thunder rolled outside. Rhea drew the curtains open. "Rain," she said.

"Our old accomplice," I smiled.

She leaned close, eyes reflecting the lightning. "Here's to swiping forward."

Raindrops streaked the glass, and the city hummed beneath us, an ordinary evening that somehow felt like a miracle.

Later, when we shut our laptops, her phone buzzed again. A new email subject blinked softly: "Congratulations, You've been matched for 365 days."

Rhea laughed. "Even the app remembers." I smiled. "Then let's keep the window open."

I wasn't talking about code or weather. I meant the window inside us , the one for listening, forgiving, staying curious, staying kind.

"Forever in beta," I whispered.

She smiled. "Perfect. Love shouldn't ever go to final release."

We laughed, knowing the app had nothing to do with it anymore. It was us , imperfect, evolving, alive.

Closing Beat

Love didn't end with a swipe or a yes. It grew into something quieter, a shared coffee, a steady laugh, a silence that healed instead of hurt.

Maybe love isn't about the perfect ending. Maybe it's about showing up, through noise, through quiet, through every small, miraculous day that feels like a restart.

Not happily ever after. Just learning how to stay, always.

End of chapter, not story. Because the app of life never really closes, it just keeps refreshing for those who dare to swipe forward.

The Cosmic Wink

(Author's Note / Epilogue)

Every love story begins with coincidence, but only the unseeing call it that.

The universe doesn't announce; it winks.

A delayed metro.

A wrong swipe.

A coffee spill that rearranges timelines.

Sometimes, all it takes is one glitch in routine for two lives to align , for a moment, or for a lifetime.

I didn't write *Wrong Swipe* as a fairy tale.

I wrote it as a mirror , to how we search for connection now: half through apps, half through courage, and almost always through confusion.

Technology may bring people together, but it's the quiet, inconvenient choices that keep them there.

Algorithms can match proximity, not presence.

Because love is still the slowest download in the fastest century.

Aarav and Rhea aren't heroes.

They're us, ambitious, distracted, sincere, flawed, learning that freedom and stability aren't rivals, but partners in the same dance.

If their story found you between versions of yourself, maybe it's the universe reminding you to update gently, not urgently.

At its heart, this story asks one question:

In a world obsessed with speed, can commitment still feel like discovery?

Because love isn't about finding someone new; it's about seeing the same person in a new light, again and again.

I've always believed every story has a twin somewhere.

For me, *Wrong Swipe* carries the same pulse as *12th Fail* , a quiet rebellion against pretending.

In that film, Manoj Kumar Sharma, a boy who once cheated his way through exams, asks a police officer how to live differently , how to become like him.

The officer gives him two words that change everything: *Stop cheating.*

Simple, but life-altering, a call to rebuild from zero, with honesty as the only rule.

Years later, after his success, Manoj returns to that same officer and says, *"I've stopped cheating."*

Aarav's moment comes on a stage, in front of a mic, where he stops performing and starts being honest, not to impress, but to be real.

Because honesty to oneself works everywhere , in love, in work, in every mission that gives life meaning.

And maybe that's where love and integrity finally meet.

If a single line here made you pause, smile, or forgive yourself a little, consider that your own cosmic wink.

Because somewhere, in the quiet corners of the internet, or the echo of a half-read message, the universe is still matching hearts.

Not perfectly, just patiently.

Truth needs silence.

Emotion needs precision.

Love just needs time that listens.

Acknowledgements

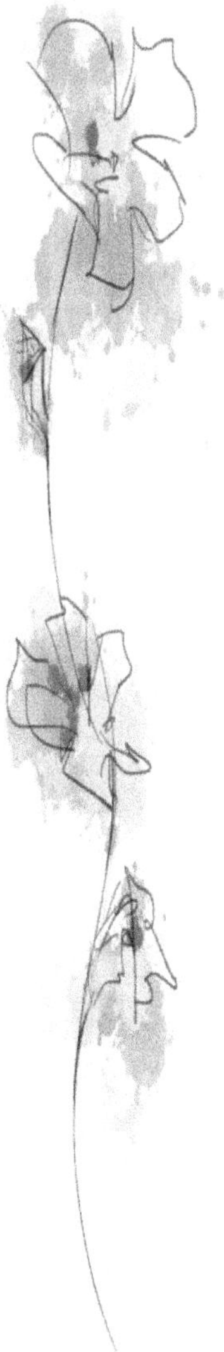

To everyone I've met, spoken to, or quietly observed, thank you for lending your emotions, contradictions, and fleeting truths to these pages.

You became the gestures, pauses, and imperfections that turned imagination into heartbeat.

To my family and friends, for grounding me with humour, patience, and faith when words faltered.

With heartfelt gratitude to filmmaker Mr. Vidhu Vinod Chopra, whose cinema has been my invisible classroom, teaching me that silence can hold truth longer than dialogue, and that emotion, when sculpted with honesty and precision, becomes timeless.

And to every reader who pauses here, thank you for listening between the lines, for completing the silences I left behind.

Verses Voyage

Reader Invitation

Aarav and Rhea's story doesn't end here. This happy ending is a new beginning with better Wi-Fi.

But what about the next chapter, the one that life writes without our permission? Five years from now, how would they balance ambition, family, friendship, fatigue, temptation, and the quiet drift that tests every long love story? Would their start-up thrive or stumble? Would laughter stay as effortless, or evolve into something quieter, wiser, realer?

If you've imagined their journey forward, I'd love to hear it. Share your reflections, sketches, or "what-if" continuations at:

connect@versesvoyage.com or

versesvoyage@gmail.com

Your thoughts will help shape the next phase of *Aarav and Rhea's* world, and contributors will be gratefully listed on the **"Thank-You Voyagers"** page at

www.VersesVoyage.com

Let's build the next chapter together.

About The Author

Verses Voyage is a traveller of hearts and moments, an observer of people, their silences, and the emotions that often go unspoken.

The writing journey began with They Left, But Their Stories Stayed : a book that listened to love and loss in their rawest forms.

With Wrong Swipe, Verses Voyage turns that same empathy toward the lighter side of connection, where humour meets honesty, and even mistakes can lead to something beautifully real.

Every story written under this name is an invitation to pause, feel, and rediscover the poetry hidden inside everyday life.

“I don’t write to invent love stories.

I write to remember how love really feels, messy, honest, and worth the wait.”

First Book

They Left, But Their Stories Stayed

15 Voices, One Grief: Stories of Love That Linger

(ASIN : B0FPRM79CL, Format: Kindle Edition)

Each story in this collection is a voice that refused to fade.

Fifteen people speak of love that ended, but never really left, of moments that still breathe in photographs, messages, and silences. Told in simple, honest words, these stories are not about death or loss alone.

They are about memory, resilience, and the quiet ways in which love continues to live, through what we remember, what we forgive, and what we carry forward.

A companion for anyone who has loved deeply and lost gently, They Left, But Their Stories Stayed reminds us that grief is not the end of love.

It's love learning to live differently.

Second Book

Wrong Swipe

A Modern Love Story in the Age of Endless Options

(**ASIN** : B0FWD4S7N9, Format Kindle Edition)

VERSES VOYAGE

www.ingramcontent.com/pod-product-compliance
Lightning Source LLC
Chambersburg PA
CBHW062138160726
48282CB00027B/863
9789334449303